LAKOTA JUSTICE

The stagecoach from the north has failed to arrive in the small settlement of Laramie, and when two men ride in fresh from a fight, the inhabitants begin to fear that the rumoured unrest among the Sioux following the discovery of gold in the Black Hills has become reality. Their concerns are relayed to the nearby fort, where visiting wagon-train scout Wes Gray agrees to join an army patrol sent to find the missing coach — but it's the first step along a trail which includes murder, kidnapping and inter-tribal warfare . . .

Books by Will DuRey
in the Linford Western Library:

THE DRUMMOND BRAND
IN THE HIGH BITTERROOTS
RETURN TO TATANKA CROSSING
A STORM IN MONTANA
LONGHORN JUSTICE
ARKANSAS BUSHWHACKERS
MEDICINE FEATHER
JEFFERSON'S SADDLE
THE GAMBLER AND THE LAW
ALONG THE TONTO RIM

WILL DuREY

LAKOTA
JUSTICE

Complete and Unabridged

LINFORD
Leicester

First published in Great Britain in 2016 by
Robert Hale
an imprint of The Crowood Press
Wiltshire

First Linford Edition
published 2019
by arrangement with
The Crowood Press
Wiltshire

A catalogue record for this book is available
from the British Library.

ISBN 978–1–4448–4271–5

Published by
F. A. Thorpe (Publishing)
Anstey, Leicestershire
Set by Words & Graphics Ltd.
Anstey, Leicestershire
Printed and bound in Great Britain by
T. J. International Ltd., Padstow, Cornwall

This book is printed on acid-free paper

1

Gold in California and the Donation Land Act grant of 320 acres of prime Oregon territory to anyone who would settle and improve it were the lures that converted the first trickle of west-bound pioneers into a surge. Undaunted by the 2,000-mile trek, men and women walked more than halfway across the continent, from the Missouri River to the Pacific Ocean, driven onward by the belief that the land of the West was their promised land. They comprised not only families who had called themselves Americans since before the Revolution, but also those who were new to the continent, for whom the vast, empty land was both a refuge from oppressive Old World regimes and an opportunity to flourish through the sweat of their own endeavour.

With their possessions loaded in long

covered wagons hauled by teams of sturdy oxen or hardworking mules, they followed the recognized trails, marking their progress as they passed each recorded landmark: Chimney Rock, South Pass, the ferry crossing-points on the Green River, Fort Hall, then west along the Humboldt to find a way across the Sierra Nevada. Many of those heading west made the journey alone, but many more organized themselves into groups, hiring men to guide them through the strange and dangerous land.

One such man for hire was Caleb Dodge, a former colonel in the Union army during the late civil war. Although he was a stern man, his reputation as wagon master was without equal. He knew that strong leadership was essential if he was to get the people in his care to their destination, and before leaving Independence he told the families of the trials that lay ahead. He listed the land, the weather, the illnesses and avoidable accidents; he told them not to overload their wagons with unnecessary gewgaws because, when the fiery heat of the Plains or the long uphill haul across the Sierra became too much for the animals, so much of what they had started with would be discarded and left to rot on the trail or adorn the tepee of some curious, acquisitive Indian.

He predicted an autumn arrival date, informing the emigrants that it would take half a year to reach their destination because they would achieve no more than fifteen miles a day and often a lot less. When they reached some of the big rivers they would only travel its width that day; crossing those rivers, Caleb insisted, would only be achieved with determination, hard work and a willingness to help each other. Everyone would need to be responsible for every wagon, families would have to help families, hauling, guiding, pushing and encouraging until every wagon had gained the far bank.

On this trip, Wes Gray, Caleb's chief

scout, hadn't been in the meeting hall to hear Caleb say those things, but he knew he'd said them. He always did. Wes had heard them many times before and now, as he sat astride his big saddle horse, Red, on a ridge above the western bank of the Blue, the evidence of Caleb's leadership lay below him. These new emigrants had overcome their first major hurdle. The last wagons were crossing the river before joining the night circle, which was forming on the plain 200 yards beyond.

The Blue wouldn't be the most difficult obstacle these pioneers would encounter, but it was here that Caleb's procedures were first put into practice, to be maintained for the trek ahead. The river wasn't fast-flowing but it was too deep for the animals to haul the long prairie schooners. So, with ropes and logs the wagons were floated and pulled, providing some men with an opportunity to demonstrate their ability to oversee the operation, others to master the engineering aspects of the job, and the remainder to add their strength to that of the beasts when hauling the wagons over the water and on to the far bank.

As arranged, Wes had met up with the wagons the night before, making himself available, along with the rest of Caleb's workforce, to help at the first river crossing. He'd worked all day, offering advice where it was needed and lending the strength in his body to haul and push whenever necessary. But now they were all across and his duty called him further afield. The wagons would travel no further this day because every one had to be checked for loose or fractured wheels, torn canvas and shifted loads. Then, when the night fires were lit, there would be a gathering, a celebration for a task achieved and a boost for the long weary days ahead.

Beyond the Blue the territory to the north was the homeland of the Lakota, the many tribes of nomadic Sioux who fished the great rivers and fed on the game that abounded in the hills. It was a fabulous land, a panorama of rolling hills and snow-topped mountains, vast expanses of flat plains, dense forests and long, fertile valleys. Wes Gray had lived west of the Missouri since his youth, had crossed the Rockies and seen the great Western Ocean, had travelled north in the great winter snows and south to the land scorched clear of plants and animals, but this was the land he loved best.

He'd set foot on this land before forts had been built and before soldiers patrolled the area; before farmers built homes and citizens built settlements. As a youth he had learned the ways of the West from no less a person than 'Blanket' Jim Bridger. Together they had set traps and hunted, then lived off the income made from the pelts of bear, deer, beaver and buffalo. They had lived in caves, cabins and tepees, sometimes alone, often with tribesmen.

Wes had an Arapaho wife, Little Feather, who lived with her people in the Snake River country where he had spent many winters. Apart from the feelings he shared with Little Feather, the marriage had been a declaration to the whole village that his relationship with them was permanent; that their needs were his needs, their enemies his enemies and their struggles his struggles.

From that point he had been a brother of the Arapaho. Not only had they taught him their spoken tongue but also the sign language common to the tribes of all the nations that wandered the Plains. They also gave him a new name, Medicine Feather. Among the nomad tribes it had become a name acknowledged with honour. Among his own people, men trod carefully when they heard the name Wes Gray.

When the last wagon closed the circle Wes turned his horse westward. Two or three hours of daylight remained, which was enough time for him to cover as much ground as the wagons would travel in a day. His duty was to scout ahead, check the trail for unexpected obstacles like swollen rivers and rock slides and, if necessary, find a safe, alternative route that wouldn't cause a vast delay. Time was important. The wagon train was scheduled to be in California in September, but delays along the 2,000 miles from Kansas were inevitable and, if the winter snows began to fall in the Sierras before the wagons crossed, the journey could end in disaster. Such a thought was the spur that drove Caleb Dodge to be a tough wagon master. Such a doubt never entered Wes Gray's mind.

If all was well, if there was nothing to impede the progress of the wagons, Wes wouldn't rejoin them for seven or eight days, not until they reached the banks of the Platte which they would follow all the way to Fort Bridger. Perhaps he'd visit Jim Taylor, a friend who had settled on a V-shaped piece of land where the Mildwater Creek met the South Platte. Meanwhile, he'd fork north to Fort Laramie where he would inform the military of the presence of this group of emigrants on the Oregon Trail. It would also be an opportunity to learn the mood of the tribes and of any possible threat of attack.

The recent discovery of gold in the northern Black Hills had brought an influx of white men to the Dakota territory, incurring the wrath of the Indians. The Paha Sapa, the Black Hills, was not only the sacred land of the Lakota people but also theirs by right as it was encompassed within the area set aside for Indian tribes in the treaty that had been signed at Fort Laramie only six years earlier. Now miners were desecrating the hills, townships were being built and white men settling on land which had been promised to the Sioux. The government, despite its words of peace, was sending soldiers to the area with threats of war if the Sioux tried to protect their property.

So far the Indians' quarrel had been with the military; Wes knew of no recent conflict with travellers along the Oregon Trail, nor of any events likely to alter matters this far south, but being aware of and preparing for such dangers was why Caleb Dodge hired him. So Wes rode on through the high, bluestem grass of that country, taking advantage of whatever high ground was available from which he could survey the land ahead, the next section of the way westward for the wagons.

Early on the following morning he came across the tracks of four unshod ponies. Sioux, he suspected, hunting or scouting for signs that the buffalo had returned. They weren't far ahead, perhaps an hour. Wes hoped to find them, pass around a pipe and, with the use of sign language and the handful of Sioux words he'd acquired, exchange news. Perhaps, if their village was close by, they would invite him to spend the night for, like the Cheyenne, the Arapaho were cousins and allies of the Sioux, so when he spoke of his family on the Snake he would be welcome in their tepees.

He came across them at a spot along the North Platte where mountain streams from both north and south plunged into the main artery, dropping from heights of thirty and forty feet, respectively. The Indians called the place The Valley Where Two Waters Fall. It was a place that Wes never tired of seeing. High banks, thronged with hickory and cottonwoods, sloped down to the river a quarter of a mile below. The grass was greener here, shorter and decorated with wild flowers of purple and yellow. Willow trees and thick, chest-high bushes provided shade at the water's edge. Apart from the turmoil caused by the upstream cascades, the river was so clear that rocks and fish within could be seen as easily as bonnets in a haberdasher's window. But the sound of the plunging water was a constant roar; songbirds sang, but a man had to become accustomed to the crash of water before he heard them.

Wes dismounted on the slope above

the riverbank to confirm the identity of the riders he had been trailing. It didn't pay to approach Indians in a hurry. It startled them. Only attacking enemies advanced at a gallop. Wes wanted to get a good look at the Indians and make his presence known before descending. In this instance his cautious approach was rewarded. As soon as he saw the markings on the ponies he realized his mistake. The four warriors were not Sioux. They were Shoshones, and the Shoshone, like the Crow, had been since time immemorial mortal enemies of the Sioux. They wouldn't welcome Wes to their camp, his Arapaho connections would be no help to him with these warriors; they were in the land of their enemies.

Wes remained hidden for several minutes, watching the four Shoshones. Scant though their clothing and armaments were, there was something almost military in the uniformity of their appearance. They wore no paint and their unbraided hair was held back by a broad, rabbit-skin band. Their clothing consisted of hide breechcloths and moccasins, and their weapons were a bow, a small animal-skin quiver full of arrows, a scalping knife in a sheath on their left hip and a stone-head axe, which was carried in the right hand. Wes had no intention of getting mixed up in an intertribal war. Those battles, with rules and behaviour that even Blanket Jim didn't fully understand, had been waged over centuries.

It occurred to him, however, that four was a small number for a raiding party. Usually they were at least twelve strong, a group small enough to move quickly but large enough to inflict damage in the event of discovery. This made Wes suspect that here was an advance group sent out to locate a likely Sioux village; that thought was swiftly followed by a question: how far behind was the main raiding party? If they were close they would already have come across his own tracks intermingled with the unshod hoof-marks of their comrades.

Certain that the Shoshone would have no mercy on him if he was found spying on them, Wes decided to move. Further along the bank, where the mountain stream tumbled into the North Platte, the terrain was high, hard rock. No tracks would be left there and, in the event of discovery, Wes could ride a little way along in the water to be sure of losing any followers. Keeping a hand over Red's muzzle he walked him back over the ridge and out of sight of the braves below.

Curiosity made him reluctant to leave the valley without observing the Shoshones for a while longer. If they were part of a larger group it was important to know how large and whether they were any kind of threat to the settlers he was leading along the Overland Trail. Once he'd gained the high ground of grey obsidian rock he circled round, looking for a suitable vantage point. Telltale markings where chunks had been hewn away to make arrow heads and tomahawk blades identified this as a popular place for the Indian nations, but Wes discounted stone gathering as the purpose of the Shoshones. They had come to raid the Sioux, steal their ponies and their women; trophies of both kinds would bring honour and wealth when they returned to their own village.

Eventually he came upon a deep cleft which provided both a hiding-place and a commanding view of the valley and its approaches. He drank deeply from his water can, then poured some into his hat for Red. He also fed the big horse a handful of oats and was biting on a chunk of dried beef when movement off to his right caught his attention. The main party had arrived. The ability of Indians to remain invisible until the last possible moment never failed to amaze him. He counted eighteen of them and, until they topped the ridge that led down to the river, he had been unaware of their approach. They knew how to use the land as camouflage. They could find gulches and ravines to ride along that dropped below ground level and out of sight of watchers. He had known ambushes on prairie land that looked flat and barren but which hid troughs and ridges so secret that a hundred Indians could wait within twenty yards of their prey without fear of discovery.

Now they were at the point where Wes had headed for the rocks. They paused, glanced in his direction but without any eagerness to follow. One white man wasn't worth their interest. They were, after all, raiders in the land of their most bitter enemies, and if they were to be successful it was essential that their presence was undetected. White men fired guns and the sound of a gunshot travelled far. Sioux warriors would investigate if such a thing should happen. The scalp of a white man was a great trophy, but not worth the risk to the successful outcome of their raid. Eventually they rode down the escarpment and joined the four who had been the advance party.

Their leader was distinguished by a

bone ornament that raised the hair on the crown of his head by four inches, creating a fold as it fell down his back. The ornament also kept a single feather in place, it being at the back of his head and hanging down so that its tip touched his shoulder. He gave instructions to his followers: two were assigned to keep watch on the trail they'd just ridden and two more were set to watching across the river. The others feasted on berries and roots found on the riverbank, and dried meat that they carried in beaded pouches on their ponies. The ponies rested in the shade or waded into the water until the Indians were ready to move on.

After the guards had been changed to allow the original watch to eat, the Indians moved out in two groups. The first, ten strong and led by the chief, walked upriver, past the cascades where, surprisingly, the water was no deeper than hock high, and they stayed in the river until they had rounded a bend and were gone from sight. The other group went back up the slope, cautiously, and disappeared again among the fissures and crevices of the terrain.

Content that the Shoshone raiders weren't a threat to the wagon train, Wes moved from his rocky hiding-place down to the grassy slopes of the valley. The sun was beginning to slip in the sky and it wouldn't be possible to reach the fort before nightfall. But there was still travelling time in the day and Wes decided to use it. He didn't want to camp in this valley in case the Shoshone had arranged to reunite here after their separate raids.

2

The new Stetson with its band of silver discs had been admired by several of Jake Welchman's friends and acquaintances, and he was inspecting it when the bullet ploughed through his temple and killed him outright. He fell from the high board of the Wells Fargo coach on to the hard trail below. The hat fluttered down beside him. Surprised by the attack and confronted by three armed men whose faces were half-covered with grubby neckerchiefs, Ben Garland hauled the team to a halt. Under threat from the outlaw leader he threw down the strongbox. One man dismounted, blasted apart the lock and, with a whistle that signified they'd hit the mother lode, began stashing the bundles of notes into saddle-bags.

Meanwhile the third man had made a new discovery, one that pleased him almost as much as the rich pickings from the strongbox. The coach was carrying a passenger, a fear-stricken girl hoping to avoid detection in the dark interior. Ellie Rogers had left her Indiana home some weeks earlier with the purpose of joining her fiancé, Captain Eugene O'Malley at military headquarters in Edwinton, but he had been posted to Fort Laramie and his telegram to stop her travelling had not arrived in time.

Now, without his knowledge, she was following him into the West, determined to become an army wife. When she was pulled from the coach and flung to the ground Ben Garland protested. Not only was she a passenger in his care, but his natural instinct was to treat females with respect. When his words fell on deaf ears he made the mistake of reaching for his gun. He suffered the same fate as his pal. In a moment he too lay dead on the road.

The outlaw leader told his cohort to leave the girl. Cavalry troops patrolled the area, so they needed to head south as quickly as possible. He turned his horse to lead the gang away, then stopped to gather up Jake's Stetson, with which he replaced his own old grey hat.

'Come on,' he called and put spur to horse. The man with the money was soon in the saddle and following, but the third man, Clem Butler, was reluctant to lose his prize.

'Perhaps there isn't time at the moment,' he told the girl, 'but you'll keep for later.' He punched her on the jaw, threw her unconscious body over his saddle, then climbed on to the horse himself.

They rode for three hours, sticking to rugged terrain, avoiding recognized trails and thus the chance of meeting other travellers, until they were well clear of the site of the hold-up. Their pace was handicapped by the fact that Clem Butler's horse carried double. Ellie had covered the first part of the journey unconscious and slung over the saddle like an over-large blanket. Then, when her senses returned to her, she was obliged by the restrictions of her dress to ride sidesaddle as Clem straddled the bareback area behind her.

Fear, evoked by the memory of the dead stage driver and shotgun guard, gripped Ellie, who had never before witnessed violent death. Her mind was tormented with visions of that hold-up and her recognition of the predicament she was in. Shock and fear caused her to tremble and gradually, just as the mental anguish of the late morning was becoming almost unbearable, so too did the effects of the physical abuse become only too evident. Aches and pains racked her body: she was suffering abrasions from having been thrown to the ground, a bruise was swelling where she'd been punched, she felt soreness across her midriff where her body had been pressed against the hard leather saddle, and nausea and dizziness from being hung head down across the horse.

Clem Butler was repulsive to her. His arms encircled her, pressed tightly against her. He exhaled his warm, unpleasant breath against her neck and ear and although she refused to turn her head in his direction she could sense the lustful looks that he cast upon her. Occasionally his hands touched her, almost casually but bearing a message of what was to befall her when they stopped. Escape, it seemed, was impossible. Her hands were tied together with a long strip of rawhide, the other end of which was secured to the pommel of Clem's saddle. If she jumped off she would be dragged along behind, and Clem, she was sure, would enjoy every minute. Nor did she expect any sympathy from the other two.

Lew Butler and Charlie Huntz had made it clear that they didn't want anything to do with her. They had cursed Clem for not leaving her at the stagecoach, where there had been the possibility of rescue. If they'd left her behind she could have unharnessed one of the horses and ridden on to the nearest settlement. Lew and Charlie didn't really care if she lived or died, but kidnap for the purpose which Clem had in mind was not their way. If a posse caught up with them now they would be shown no pity. Abusing a woman got a man hanged as surely as rustling cattle or stealing a horse. Now Clem's horse was blowing hard with the effort of keeping up but it was necessary to put more distance between themselves and the hold-up.

All three outlaws had, as soon as they were clear of the stricken stagecoach, removed the neckerchiefs that covered the lower part of their faces. Although Lew was broader and two inches taller than Clem, it was clear to anyone who met them that they were brothers. Even Lew's heavy jowls couldn't distract attention from the long, straight nose they had in common, nor the thick eyebrows over long-lashed brown eyes. These features and the dark, lank hair confirmed they were brothers. Charlie Huntz had an unruly mass of red hair and a full red beard through which his tongue continuously flicked as it tried to moisten his thin dry lips. His small blue eyes were restless, forever searching for what might be approaching, never settling on what was within reach.

At about the time that the coach should have been reaching the trading post near Fort Laramie the group halted on a ridge above a stream, a tributary of the North Platte. Satisfied that the area was clear of both white men and Indians, Lew Butler led the way down to the water's edge. The horses dipped their heads to drink. Clem unfastened the rawhide strip from the saddle horn and pushed Ellie out of the saddle. With a painful yelp she landed half-in and half-out of the stream, her head cracking against a submerged rock. Clem grinned at her distress.

'Well,' he said, dismounting, 'guess it's time.' He grinned at Ellie as she wiped the water from her face.

'Ain't you interested in how much we got?' Charlie Huntz, who had exchanged an anxious glance with Lew, tried to distract Clem from his purpose. He rubbed his hand around his neck as though he could already feel a rope noose tightening there.

'You count it,' said Clem. 'Just give me my share and perhaps I'll let you have a share of this one.' Ellie tried to pull away from him but he'd wrapped the strap of rawhide several times around his left wrist. 'No good,' he told her. 'You can't get away.' He tugged suddenly and swiftly, pulling Ellie off balance so that she stumbled towards him. When he tried to kiss her she pushed him away.

'Come on, Clem,' said Lew. He was following Charlie Huntz further up the bank to where he was emptying the contents of his saddle-bags. 'I've never seen so much money at one time.'

'And it's all ours,' Charlie shouted gleefully.

Clem turned his head that way and seemed bemused by the number of bundles scattered at Charlie's feet. 'What do you think we got there?'

'Don't know,' said his brother, 'and don't care, either.'

'Must have been a special bank run,' declared Charlie. He was checking the value of the bundles and forming them into three piles. 'Bring your saddlebags, Clem, if you want a share.'

Clem looked at Ellie, torn for a moment between his desire for her and his love of money. He grinned, drew a long knife from a scabbard on his left hip and tied the length of rawhide to it. Then he plunged the blade into the ground.

'Be good,' he told Ellie. He left her by the water while he led his horse up to where the other two were sharing a joke about the money.

'More than eighty thousand dollars,' declared Charlie. 'We'll be the kings of Cheyenne.'

'No,' said Lew. 'We can't go to

Cheyenne with this money. Where would we have got eighty thousand dollars? Sheriff Boyston would have us in jail before we'd laid down our first full house. No, Charlie. We gotta go somewhere we ain't known. Some big city.'

'St Louis,' said Clem.

'New Orleans,' said Charlie. 'Always did want to take me a ride on one of those riverboats. Hear tell they got show girls and minstrels on board to entertain people while they're playing the gambling tables.'

Lew smiled. 'Sounds good,' he said, 'but I've got a hankering for San Francisco. I'd like to see the ocean.'

'Lots of things I'd like to see,' said Charlie Huntz.

With such talk combined with the pleasurable employment of filling their saddle-bags, Ellie Rogers was momentarily forgotten. She, however, conscious that this might be her only opportunity to escape, was pulling the knife from the turf. She had no plan in her head other than to get away from the three men. Across the stream there was an abundance of hickory bushes and willow trees. If she could reach them before they noticed she'd gone then perhaps there was a chance they would ride away without her. Lew and Charlie, she knew, were anxious to be free of her. Only Clem would mount any kind of a search, but it wouldn't be for long. They needed to get as far away as possible from the stagecoach hold-up.

Clem thought the knife was stuck securely in firm ground, but the stream had been much wider during the spring flood and beneath the grassy surface the soil was still moist and loose. Even for Ellie, for whom physical strength had never been a necessary development, the knife came free without much effort. She glanced at her captors who were still in a happy huddle thirty yards away. Partly obscured from their sight by the grazing horses, she moved towards the water, slowly at first, then, when her departure seemed to be unobserved, she began to hurry across to the other side.

She had almost gained the far side of the stream when Clem spotted her attempted escape. Instantly he was running down the slope, splashing through the water, and had her by the arm before she had taken more than six steps on the opposite bank. Even though she still held the knife in her tethered hands, she offered no immediate resistance. Panic constricted her breathing and, gulping for air, she allowed Clem to take the weapon from her and pull her back across the water.

She stumbled once, sinking to her knees in the stream. The chill of the running water released the tension in her body. She sobbed, her misery expelled in a heavy sigh which freed the tightness in her chest. She screamed, an instinctive declaration of fear but also of defiance. Her shrieks and struggles continued as Clem dragged her up the bank, yelling as loudly as she could, pleading for mercy which she knew he would never show.

'Shut her up, can't you,' called Lew. 'They'll hear her in Fort Laramie if she keeps up that din.'

Clem grinned at her; he pushed his arm across his chest to deliver her a backhand blow, but he never landed it. Instead, his eyes bulged with surprise and unuttered pain, then he pitched forward, fell against her, knocking her to the ground, pinning her there with the weight of his body.

The things that happened next all happened together. The realization that two arrows protruded from Clem's back and that he was now a dead weight on top of her, registered with Ellie at the same time as the wild whoops and sounds of splashing came from the direction of the river. She heard someone, Charlie Huntz she suspected, shout, 'Indians!' That immediately followed by the crash of gunfire. At that moment, for Ellie the world consisted of nothing but shouts and the pounding of hoofs.

Suddenly an Indian was above her, leaping from a painted, white pony and brandishing a huge knife. His face was squat and dark with a flat nose and narrow eyes. It was painted with blue lines and yellow splotches and Ellie thought he was a devil risen from Hell itself. His eyes met hers but his expression didn't alter. He grabbed the hair on Clem's head and with a swift single swipe of the knife sliced off the top. Blood drizzled on to Ellie's face and the Indian shouted a victory cry as he held the scalp aloft. But at that very moment of his triumph a bullet tore through his body and he dropped, writhing, to the ground.

Gripped as she was by terror, it took Ellie several moments to realize that the turmoil had receded, that the gun battle had moved away from the river-bank. Presently, the only sounds she could hear were the rippling of the water over the stony riverbed and the song of those birds that now found it safe enough to resume their natural life.

For Ellie, however, nothing was natural. Supine and bound, she feared she would suffocate where she lay. The weight of Clem's body, which covered her from head to toe, seemed to increase moment by moment. She felt as though she was being pressed into the ground. All the air had been driven from her lungs and she could manage only short, shallow breaths, each one as painful as a knife thrust.

But the human spirit is indomitable and Ellie's desire to survive was intact. Instinct told her that she had to get out from under Clem's body and find a refuge before anyone came back. Indian or white man, whoever it was would kill her. By manoeuvring her legs she figured she'd be able to work herself into a position which would give her more purchase to turn her body and slide out. Once free of Clem's weight she could find the knife and cut her bonds.

As it happened, her first significant

movement was with her shoulders. Squirming with her buttocks to move her legs caused a corresponding, involuntary lift with the upper part of her body. It wasn't enough to free any part of her but it did cause Clem's head to roll from her chest to her shoulder. His wide open eyes stared at her, the blood from his lifted scalp running thickly down his face in twin rivulets. The ugliness revolted her and she heaved again with her body until the pain in her arms bade her stop.

She hadn't achieved much physically, but it provided the mental boost she needed to continue to struggle, She was convinced that she was capable of freeing herself from the burden of Clem's body. What she wasn't sure about was how long it would take her, whether she had time to escape before her tormentors or the Indians returned.

It took several minutes, alternately heaving with her shoulders then quirming with her buttocks to free her legs. This achieved, she bent them at the knees in preparation for a final effort. With the lower part of her body unrestricted she hoped to be able to relax the strain on her arms and, by kneeling and turning, get out of the situation she was in.

First though, she needed a moment to revive from her exertions so far. She had been beaten, restrained, deprived of food and water and had witnessed such violence as she had hardly supposed possible; now she feared that if she didn't escape from this place she wouldn't survive to the end of the day. Her chest ached from the very act of breathing and her arms felt as though they were close to leaving their sockets. Still, Ellie convinced herself that one last effort would see her free. She moved her legs in readiness, giving herself room to twist which would provide sufficient purchase to turn her torso. Then something sticky and hairy clamped around her right ankle and gripped tightly.

Ellie gasped and turned her head.

The Indian she had thought dead held her with his left hand. It also held Clem's scalp. The stickiness on her leg was Clem's blood. In his right hand the warrior still held the knife he'd used to lift Clem's scalp. For several seconds they looked at each other. No sound passed between them. Terror was the expression etched on Ellie's face. His was set with determination, eyes wide and staring, and mouth partly open.

Then he began to move. Inching forward, his expression remained unchanged, his eyes never leaving Ellie's face. She kicked out, hoping to shake herself free of his grip but succeeded only in wrenching her arms and causing herself more pain. He wasn't a big man, wiry thin, but his hand was hard on her leg and his hold growing ever tighter. She kicked out again, blanking out her mind to the agony it caused to her arms, but that effort had no more success than her first. The Indian used his right forearm to lever his chest and shoulders from the ground, then shifted his weight to his left arm. Pressing down on Ellie's ankle he pulled himself forward to within striking distance and raised the knife.

Ellie knew she was at his mercy. There was nothing more she could do. She began to imagine the searing pain as the long, broad blade sliced its way to her lungs and other organs. Or perhaps he would crawl closer still and slit her throat. They locked eyes and, for what seemed like an eternity, they stayed in those positions. Then, suddenly, the Indian's mouth disgorged an eruption of blood. It covered Ellie's dress. She screamed, then watched mesmerized as the hate-filled eyes turned blank and the Indian's head drooped forward, slowly, his forehead finally coming to rest on her thigh.

Tearfully, her body shaking with shock, she found the strength to ease herself out from under Clem. Shuddering, she knew not whether from fear or relief, she began to crawl away, then remembered the knife in the Indian's hand. She prised it from his fingers and stuck the blade into the ground, far enough to enable her to rub her rawhide bindings along the edge until they were severed.

Wiping tears from her face she tried to force her brain to decide what to do next. She didn't know where she was. She didn't know which direction would lead her to Fort Laramie or any other settlement. All she could be sure of was that she had to get away from this place. She looked across the river. That was the direction in which they'd been heading and the direction from which the Indians had attacked. She couldn't decide whether either of those facts was favourable to her. Perhaps she ought to follow the stream. It was sure to lead to a larger river. She'd be bound to come across settlers if she followed the river.

Her decision made, she determined to move on to higher ground, up to the tree line, which would give her some protection if anyone came looking for her. When she turned her heart plunged. Not ten paces from her an Indian sat astride a brown piebald pony. He was naked except for the merest deerskin cloth. His hair was loose but adorned with two eagle feathers which were worn at the back of his head. He held a round, buffalo-skin shield in his left hand and a long lance in his right. His face and body were unpainted but his horse had many markings in red and yellow. For several seconds horse and rider remained motionless, then, slowly at first, they started towards her. A sob burst from Ellie's throat. She had no more resistance.

3

When the Indians came racing across the river Charlie Huntz had his hands full of dollar bills. Hundreds of them, in tidy bundles, were wrapped inside bands denoting the Cattlemen's Bank of Chicago. So greedily was he eyeing the money that it took several seconds for the threat from beyond the narrow stream to register in his mind. By the time he'd shouted a warning — the single word — 'Indians!' arrows were already flying.

Carelessly he dropped the bundle in his right hand to enable him to grab the bulging saddle-bags from the ground, and, because his life depended on it, he ran to his horse more quickly than anyone would have thought his thickset body capable of. In one fluid movement he flung the saddle-bags over the horse's back and drew his rifle from the saddle boot. He began firing, indiscriminately, a token show of resistance with little chance of hitting the enemy.

The attackers were experienced guerrilla fighters, lying flat along the backs of their ponies to make themselves the smallest targets possible. Indeed, for some of those with rifles, their animal provided almost total protection as they clung to one flank and fired under its neck.

Lew Butler had been regarding the antics of his brother with anger. There was a code in the West with regard to the treatment of women which you ignored at your peril. Clem should have left the girl at the stagecoach. Molesting her was a greater crime than robbery and they would all be judged guilty of it no matter what little part Charlie Huntz and he had played. Perhaps it didn't matter; now that she had seen all their faces there was only one thing to be done with her when Clem was finished. If they were caught they would hang for the murder of the stagecoach driver and guard anyhow, but it sat ill with Lew that people would think of him as an abuser of women. He glanced in their direction. He had to admit his brother had been right about one thing. She was certainly pretty. Beating her ugly, as Clem seemed prepared to do, didn't make any sense.

Then, as though pushed forward by a giant's hand, Clem fell forward, his torso covering the girl. As with Ellie, the appearance of the arrows in his brother's back, the war whoops of the attacking warriors and Charlie Huntz's cry of 'Indians!' all registered at the same moment.

'Clem!' Lew shouted, even though he knew it would be to no avail. His brother was dead. He pulled his revolver from its holster and fired two wild shots in the direction of the attackers. Like Charlie, he knew the only things that could save him now were his rifle and a fast horse. Unlike Charlie, he mounted first but before he could spur his horse forward a hideous cry rose above the tumult of battle.

Lew twisted in the saddle. Standing above his brother's body, with arms raised aloft, was one of the braves. In one hand he held a knife, in the other a bloody scalp.

'Clem!' Lew shouted again, his voice taut with a hundred emotions as he witnessed the mutilation of his brother. He drew his rifle and shot at the Indian, hitting him in the back and pitching him face first on to the ground. An arrow flew close to his head, cutting short any sense of fulfilled vengeance. Survival, now, was his only thought.

'Come on, Charlie,' he shouted, 'let's ride.'

Charlie had his horse running before he was on its back. Gripping his rifle and the saddle horn he vaulted into leather as his mount followed Lew's up the ridge towards the tree line. Pursued by yelling Indians, the air buzzing with arrows and bullets, Lew and Charlie pushed their steeds to their best speed. If the white men had hoped the trees would provide sufficient cover for them to make a stand against their attackers they were soon disabused of such a notion. The trees were nothing more than an isolated line which the riders left behind almost before they knew they had reached them. Before them was an expanse of long-grassed prairie which offered them no obvious defensive position. All that remained was to try to outrun their pursuers.

For three miles the conflict ensued. The horses of the stagecoach robbers had the initial advantage. They were bigger and faster and already had a head start, but after the first mile that advantage disappeared. The Indian ponies were accustomed to long treks, were bred for it, and they carried a lot less weight. Their near-naked riders rode without heavy leather saddles, nor were they burdened with so many accoutrements as were their enemies. The gap between the two groups was maintained for another mile but then, gradually, it began to close. Bullets and arrows whistled nearer as Lew and Charlie tried to urge another burst of speed from their failing horses.

Charlie turned in the saddle several times to discharge his rifle at the band of Indians behind them. It was a waste of ammunition; his chance of hitting a target was remote at best. The Indians themselves, nine in total, had stopped yelling, content in the knowledge that they were running down their prey. They fired more frequently but they had the advantage of having their targets in view at all times. Lew peered ahead, his eyes desperately scanning for suitable cover. Unable to see any and with his horse rapidly failing to maintain its speed he knew there only remained one course of action.

'We've got to make a stand,' he yelled at Charlie. 'Get down behind the horses.'

Charlie nodded his agreement. He knew his horse couldn't go much further and, reluctant though he was to dismount, he knew that afoot, their marksmanship would improve immensely. Lew and he were more than adequate in the use of firearms; they'd lived by their guns most of their life.

Simultaneously they reined back their mounts and were off them before they came to a halt. The beasts were snorting and stamping and sweating, but their duty wasn't done. Each man grabbed his horse's bridle, pulling down on it and across, forcing the animal on to its front knees then on to its side. But by now the nearest Indians were almost upon the two white men. Lew raised his rifle and fired twice. Both the Indians fell, disappearing from sight in the long grass. Their riderless ponies galloped past.

Charlie was on one knee behind his horse, using it as a living rampart, waiting for the onrushing Indians. He could hear them now, they'd restarted their war whoops, sensing that the white men were at their mercy. Charlie felt vulnerable. Being low to the ground was a disadvantage, not least because the long grass prevented him seeing the attackers until they were almost upon him. He waited, rifle at his shoulder.

The drumming of hoofs got louder. Then a head and shoulders appeared almost above him. Instinctively he fired. The Indian hurled a spear. Neither missile found its mark but as the ridden pony hurdled the recumbent horse Charlie fired again. The slug bored a way through the Indian's head, entering under the chin, passing through the cavity of his mouth and rising into the density of his brain. He dropped at Charlie's feet, legs twitching twice before a final stillness settled over him.

Charlie only had time to recognize that that was one Indian who wouldn't be a trouble to him again when another hard-ridden pony loomed into view. Its rider released an arrow, which thudded deep into the belly of Charlie's horse. The beast jerked and rasped out a pain-filled, frightened cough. Charlie fired his rifle, three times in swift succession. Blood spurted from the Indian's chest as he tumbled backwards from his pony.

Lew, too, had his hands full. After his dispatching of the first two Indians, bullets screamed through the air from the rifles of two others who were riding wide on his left. All he could see was their wild-eyed ponies and the smoke drifting up from the barrels of the rifles which had been fired under their neck. Lew didn't fire at them. He could, perhaps, have brought down the animals but that would only be a disadvantage to Charlie and him. A combination of mounted and dismounted Indians would soon see them overpowered. Unhorsed Indians would lead to hand-to-hand fighting and, if it came to that, while heavily outnumbered he and Charlie couldn't win. Their deaths would be slow and painful. Better to go down fighting, be killed quickly by a bullet or an arrow.

Out of the long grass rode another brave. His hair was raised from the crown of his head by a bone ornament and his face was marked with two yellow lines that ran from cheek to cheek across his nose. As his pony leapt over the prostrate form of Lew's horse his arm swung in a violent arc, a tomahawk clutched in his hand. With his attention focused on the wide riders, Lew had no time to bring his rifle round to fire at the new attacker. Instead, he bent low, hoping to avoid the deadly swipe and so give himself the opportunity to draw a bead on his attacker as he passed. Unfortunately, he didn't get low enough. The flat blade of the tomahawk smacked against the crown of Lew's head, pitching him face down on to the ground.

Seeing his companion on the ground, Charlie aimed at the back of the man who had felled him. He pulled the trigger. There was an ominous, empty click. He jerked the mechanism and tried again. The result was the same. He dropped the rifle, drew his six-gun and fired two shots at the receding Indian.

Charlie grunted with satisfaction when he saw the tomahawk fall from the man's right hand. The brave grabbed at that shoulder with his left hand, brushing against the single feather that hung there.

Knowing the Indian was now out of distance for his handgun, Charlie picked up Lew's rifle and sighted along the barrel. He fired only one shot but it struck home. With arms flung wide the Indian's body bent backwards in an unnatural arc. Almost gracefully he toppled from his pony and lay still on the ground.

Charlie turned his attention to the remaining Indians. Only four remained, gathered in a line ready to recharge their quarry. Five of their comrades lay dead around the white man's makeshift defences but this latest death had a dramatic effect on them. For several moments they conferred, moments during which Charlie reloaded his rifle. But the fight was over. One of the four rode slowly forward to collect the body of their last fallen comrade; their leader, Charlie supposed. Then, at funereal pace, they rode away. Charlie pulled Lew's horse to its feet, then climbed on its back and stood in the saddle so that he was able to see them ride away, confirming the fact that the warriors had had enough.

Lew began to moan. Charlie got down, collected a water canteen from the saddle of his dying horse and poured a little of the contents over his partner's face. There was a split in Lew's skull: nothing too serious but he'd lost some blood and his hair was sticky with it. For the moment, it would have to stay that way; there wasn't enough water in the canteen to justify washing his head. While Lew came to his senses Charlie picketed his horse a few yards from where they'd made their stand. There was only one thing to be done with his own horse and he didn't want to spook Lew's when he did it.

It was a full hour before Lew felt able to travel. Even then his head was still pounding but they couldn't hang around any longer. If the Indians came back for their dead they would probably bring more braves with them. Lew and Charlie thought it unlikely they'd be able to fight them off a second time.

They determined to head for the nearest outpost, Fort Laramie. Even though it should have been the next stop for the stagecoach they'd robbed, they figured there was no reason for anyone to suspect that they were responsible. They'd be coming in from a different direction and they'd been attacked by Indians. Lew had a dead brother and Charlie a dead horse to prove it. But they wouldn't get to Fort Laramie before nightfall; with only one horse progress would be slow.

As night fell they lost that horse, too, its leg breaking when it stumbled into a gopher hole hidden by the long grass. On another day the loss of their animals and equipment would have been a cause for concern, as it was they were in high spirits from having survived a skirmish with Indians and, too, they had money-filled saddle-bags. Any grumbling they did was solely about the inconvenience of having to carry their own saddle-bags and weapons.

The thought of replacing his gear was a source of pleasure for Charlie. He was thinking about the fancy rig he'd once seen used by a Mexican caballero. The cantle and pommel with its silver-topped horn were high, so that the whole saddle looked like a comfortable seat. The leathers were wide, patterned and interlaced with silver ornaments. Charlie had admired it as soon as he saw it and, had the owner not been surrounded by a dozen of his own vaqueros at the time, he would have been happy enough to kill the man for it.

They walked in silence for several miles, Charlie's thoughts occupied with ways to spend his money while Lew was making plans of a more practical nature. Eventually he spoke.

'When we get to the fort we tell them

we've just finished trail-herding to Abilene and now we're heading for Wyoming, where we hear tell there are a lot of big ranches looking for cowboys. Indians attacked us out on the Plains and we lost everything but what we're carrying. Best not to mention Clem. If anyone comes across the bodies of him and the girl we don't want them tying us in with them. Once it's discovered that the stagecoach has been robbed and a passenger kidnapped it won't take the law long to figure out it's her.'

'What about the money?' asked Charlie, his mind preoccupied with fancy rigs and dance-hall girls. 'Do we split it now?'

'No. We can't go into Laramie with such a stash. What we'll do is take a bundle each, like it's our payoff at the end of a profitable cattle drive, but the rest we'll hide and collect after we've rested up a few days and got ourselves fitted out with horses and equipment.'

By now they'd left behind the long

grass and were on the gentle slopes of the higher ground looking for a watercourse that they could follow to the North Platte. It was almost total darkness when they found what they were looking for.

'Let's bed down here for a few hours,' said Lew, whose head was aching from the blow he'd taken. 'We'll get under way again at first light.'

Charlie agreed. Charlie always agreed with Lew. Lew was a thinker and a planner and they hadn't yet come to harm. Well, mused Charlie, there was Clem, of course, but if Clem hadn't disobeyed Lew by bringing along the girl they never would have crossed paths with those Indians and Clem wouldn't be dead. No, he thought, it wasn't Lew's fault. If they hadn't been slowed down by the girl they would have been miles away from that riverbank. He sniffed, audibly, then stopped.

'Smoke,' he said softly.

The same thought occurred to both

outlaws. In this wilderness, where there was smoke there were people and where there were people there were horses. Lew rubbed his face hoping to wipe away the nagging pain, then ushered Charlie ahead. Though the sky was clear of clouds, the waning moon cast little light on the land and Lew and Charlie moved ahead stealthily, crawling along the ground to draw close to a stand of cottonwoods they'd identified as the likely location of a campfire.

Now and then a night breeze fluttered, stirring the foliage, carrying the sound of fast-flowing water from the stream below. Lew motioned for Charlie to hold his position while he moved to the other side of the dell in which the cottonwoods grew. As he was circling in a wide arc he came across two ponies. They were tethered on the far side of the grove, near the river. One, a dull grey, turned its head in Lew's direction. The other, light-coloured with feathers tied in its mane and paint-marks on its flanks and legs, gave a nervous snicker.

Alerted by the pony's warning the two people sitting cross-legged by the small fire reached for their bows and arrows. They stood and moved in the direction of their ponies.

Behind them, Charlie Huntz stepped into the clearing.

'Horses,' he said 'Just what we're looking for and guess what, you ain't gonna need them any more.' He pulled the trigger, once, twice and the two boys, for indeed they could have been no older than fourteen, died where they fell.

4

Wes Gray rode into Fort Laramie before noon and stepped down from his big horse outside the office of the commanding officer. He was no stranger to the fort. On more than one occasion he'd been hired by the army to act as guide for an expedition or translator at a parlay with an Indian tribe. His knowledge and skills were legendary, his advice, especially on Indian affairs, always sought.

Wes smacked his broad-brimmed hat against his leg to loosen the dust that had collected during his ride. He stepped on to the porch and paused, took a look around the outpost to familiarize himself with its layout. In terms of buildings, nothing much had changed in the year since his last visit, but, to his surprise, there were more soldiers in evidence. He figured it could simply mean that there were fewer out on patrol but it troubled him that the increase was more likely a show of force designed to further Washington's desire to push the tribesmen on to reservations.

He opened the office door and stepped into a room which, in contrast to the glare and heat of the sun outside, was dark and cool. A sergeant, seated behind a cluttered desk, looked up from the pile of documents he was checking.

'As I live and breathe,' he exclaimed, 'Wes Gray. What are you doing back here? Bringing through more settlers?'

'That's right. Got a wagon train heading for California. Thought I'd drop by and pay my compliments to the colonel.' Wes's reasons for coming into the fort weren't purely social. Letting the army know they were in the vicinity meant that patrols in the area would keep an eye on them and pass on any information that could affect their safety.

The sergeant stood and rapped with his knuckles on a door behind his desk. Without waiting for an answer he opened it.

'Wes Gray out here, sir.'

'Send him in, Sergeant.' Colonel Flint was a trim man in middle-age. His hair was short and dark as was the moustache and beard that encircled his mouth. His eyes, too, were small and dark but gave the impression of a man alert to his surroundings. His smile of welcome was genuine when he saw the buckskin-clad scout.

After exchanging greetings, Colonel Flint confirmed Wes's initial impression. The regular troops of the Fourth Infantry had been augmented by a company of the Second Cavalry.

'The fort is bursting with men,' he announced. Wes asked the obvious question.

'Are you expecting trouble?'

Colonel Flint shook his head. 'Nothing imminent but we need to be prepared. There are signs of increasing unrest among those bands hostile to the idea of settling on a reservation. Further north there's been several incidents with miners. Some have been killed.'

'Miners shouldn't be in the Black Hills. That's Sioux land.'

Colonel Flint exhaled loudly as though he'd been holding his breath a long time.

'There's gold there, Wes. An agreement isn't going to hold back the prospectors.'

'That's the army's job, isn't it?'

'The army's job is to do what government orders it to do, And we're ordered to protect the miners.'

'Even though it was the army generals who signed their names to the treaty six years ago?'

'I know where your loyalties lie, Wes. Perhaps it won't come to a war. Those tribes that remain along the Platte seem content. Sometimes a band of Sioux or Cheyennes come to the fort to trade. There's no trouble while they're here.

From the hills they watch the wagons that pass through their land but there hasn't been any aggression. No reason why that should change.'

'I saw a party of Shoshones yesterday,' said Wes, 'about half a day south of here.' He told Colonel Flint what he'd seen along the North Platte. Colonel Flint rubbed his jaw.

'Bit far east for Shoshones, wouldn't you say?'

'They weren't anywhere near the wagon trail so I figured they were on a raiding trip against the Sioux. Probably after horses.'

'Seems likely,' said the CO.

Wes was about to ask about the terrain ahead, if the rivers were crossable or if any trails had been blocked by winter landslides, when the sergeant opened the door again.

'Mr Clayport to see you, Colonel.'

Curly Clayport worked for Wells Fargo. He was supervisor of the stage depot in the civilian settlement a couple of miles from the fort, and the epitome of a key Wells Fargo employee — energetic, astute and prepared to put the needs of the company before all else. He was a broad-shouldered man, not quite six feet tall, clean-shaven and devoid of most of the hair from the middle of his head.

He came into the room on the heels of the sergeant. Wes and he had met on several occasions and liked each other, but the Wells Fargo man was barely able to acknowledge the scout's presence, so eager was he to speak to Colonel Flint. His movement was brisk, his words tumbled out like rocks in a landslide.

'Colonel, we've got a problem. The stage from Deadwood hasn't arrived. It should have been here late afternoon yesterday.'

Unflustered, Colonel Flint gave his opinion.

'Coach timetables aren't my affair, Mr Clayport. Won't be the first time the coach has been delayed by a lame horse or a broken wheel. No doubt it'll turn up in due course.'

'I suspect it's more serious than that, Colonel. I think it's been attacked by Indians.'

'Indians! Now what makes you think that?'

'Because two men have just ridden into the settlement who are lucky to still have hair on their heads.'

'What men?'

'Strangers. Came in from the south. Riding Indian ponies because their own mounts were killed in the attack. They claim they fought off a dozen of the devils in the long-grass country.'

'I rode in from the south,' said Wes, 'and the only warlike band I saw was a party of Shoshones. They weren't travelling quickly enough to have attacked a stagecoach north of here and then fight those men in the south.'

He rubbed his jaw. Any hint of hostilities was bad news for everyone who hoped to settle in the area and for the people crossing the continent in wagons. He also knew that it was common practice to blame the tribes for any misdeed. Not that he was laying such an accusation against Curly: the Wells Fargo man was simply worried about a stagecoach for which he was responsible and repeating what two strangers had told him.

'Might be interesting to hear their story,' Wes suggested. 'Find out why they were attacked.'

'I'd agree with you, Wes, if we were laying blame for both attacks on the same group, but that ain't the way of it. Weren't Shoshones that attacked those men,' said Clayport, 'those were Sioux ponies they were riding. This is Sioux country. If the stagecoach has been attacked by Indians then it could mean a full-scale uprising.'

Such a thought brought an instant response from Colonel Flint.

'Sergeant, get Captain O'Malley here at once.'

O'Malley was given instructions to take six men and ride the trail towards Deadwood to find out what had befallen the stagecoach.

'Then report straight back here. But first,' said Colonel Flint, 'question those two men at the settlement. Find out all you can about that attack.'

'Do you mind if I tag along,' asked Wes Gray. 'If there's trouble brewing I need to warn Caleb as soon as possible.'

Neither Colonel Flint nor Captain O'Malley had any objection, so Wes remounted Red and rode side by side with the captain to the settlement. Other than a few words of introduction they rode in silence.

It came as no surprise to either man to find that the two Indian ponies were tied to the hitching rail outside Jed Clancy's store. Clancy's store was the biggest building in the settlement and served a dual purpose. The larger part was a store that stocked dry goods and provisions, clothing and farming equipment, guns and ammunition, and acted as a barter post for the outlying farms. The other part was a saloon with a high counter and room for four small tables.

Clancy and his wife ran the enterprise between them, each fulfilling the roles of storekeeper and bartender as required. Their services were also retained by Wells Fargo to provide food and whatever comfort they could for the stagecoach passengers. The arrival of a full stagecoach was the only time all four tables were in use.

Before stepping inside, Wes looked over the ponies at the rail. He recognized the paint markings on the animals and the designs on the blankets over their backs as typical Sioux.

Three men lounged against the bar behind which both Jed Clancy and his wife stood. Two of the four tables were occupied. At one was slumped a solitary man, unconscious, his head, shoulders and arms resting on the table, a part-empty whiskey bottle close to his right hand and a part-full glass near his left.

A poker game was in progress at the other table although, truth be told, the five men seated around it and those standing on both sides of the counter were more engrossed in conversation than in the turn of the cards. The subject under discussion was Indians. The death of a handful at the hands of two resourceful newcomers was a cause for celebration and boasting, but the sudden appearance of a cavalry officer in their midst brought the conversation to an abrupt halt.

Lew Butler and Charlie Huntz were among the five playing poker. When questioned by Captain O'Malley they stuck to the story they'd concocted along the trail. They were cattle drovers from Abilene hoping to find work in Wyoming. Without warning they had been attacked by a bunch of Indians. Their horses were shot from under them but they managed to fight off the attack by killing most of the Indians. They had rounded up a couple of ponies and made their way to Laramie, knowing there was a fort near by.

When O'Malley seemed satisfied with their story Wes Gray asked some questions of his own.

'What were they after?'

Charlie Huntz looked quizzically at the scout and pushed a stubby hand through his unruly red hair.

'After? Our scalps, I suppose.'

'Ain't it enough that we're white and they're Indian?' asked Lew.

'Not usually. Most times they're after some sort of prize, something to take back to the village that will increase their own wealth and importance.'

'Such as?'

'Such as pelts or weapons or horses. Did you have pack animals with you?'

'No,' said Charlie.

'I told you,' said Lew, his voice betraying annoyance at Wes's questions, 'we're cattlemen moving on to Wyoming. We had nothing but the horses under us and the clothes we're still wearing.'

Wes looked at the pile of dollar notes in front of each man. If the two men had travelled north without much in the way of goods they certainly had a sizeable bankroll. Still, their story of having recently completed a trail drive could account for that. He knew that drovers on long drives earned good pay. If these two hadn't squandered it on women and whiskey they were a rare breed, but it happened.

'Perhaps they were after our horses,' said Charlie.

'If that was the case it's unlikely they'd shoot them. Not much honour in dragging a dead horse back to the village.'

'Don't suppose they intended to kill the horses. Likely they were aiming for us. Horse just got in the way of the arrows.'

'You don't know the Sioux. If your horses were the prize they were never in any danger of being hit by an arrow.'

Lew was becoming edgy. Charlie was a good man, a good friend, but he didn't always think before speaking. The fellow in buckskin was beginning to make Charlie grope for answers, provide an explanation which he didn't have. Any minute now Charlie was likely to say something incompatible with the story they'd told. He growled at Wes.

'Are you calling us liars?'

Wes noted the other's tone. 'No. Trying to find a reason for the attack. There's been no trouble with tribes for some time so we need to know what's riled them. If this is an isolated incident then it'll help to know what caused it. We don't want it escalating into something bigger. War with the Sioux isn't good for anyone.'

Jed Clancy spoke up. 'Don't think it is an isolated incident, Wes. The Deadwood stage hasn't arrived. Seems likely the Sioux have hit that, too.'

'You're jumping to conclusions, Jed. Nobody knows what's happened to the coach. The captain and his troopers are heading north now to investigate.'

'Seems to me,' said Lew Butler, 'that you're mighty keen to prove the Indians innocent.'

'No. Just keen to prove the innocent

innocent. It don't pay to decide in advance who did what. When we find the stagecoach we'll find out what happened.'

'We told you what happened to us,' said Charlie. 'We got attacked without reason. Our dead horses and a bunch of dead Indians are lying out there in the long-grass country to prove it.'

Dead horses maybe, thought Wes, but no dead Indians. Their comrades would have been back for the bodies. And anyhow, dead bodies would only prove there had been a fight, not the cause of it. Lew Butler spoke.

'The army should be out there killing all of them. Murderous devils. There ain't none of them should be left alive.' As he spoke he sensed a sudden change of atmosphere in the room, a sensation that he'd said something dangerous. He couldn't think what it could be. He'd expressed the same sentiment earlier when recounting details of the fight to the gathered citizens.

But Wes Gray wasn't a stranger to the

people who lived near Fort Laramie. His history was well known. Now, as he straightened up, his shoulders seemed to broaden and his arms to relax as they hung by his side, his right hand lying carelessly close to his revolver.

'That's a mean attitude,' he said to Lew Butler. 'There are good Indians and bad Indians just as there are good whites and bad.'

'Yeah? Well, I've never met any good Indians. They're all blood-lusting, pox-riddled curs. The world would be a better place if they were all swept from it.'

The silence in the room was intensified by the ticking of a sturdy cabinet clock on the wall behind the counter. When Wes spoke his voice was low but carried a threat that made some men move away from the table where Lew Butler sat.

'My wife is Arapaho.'

For some moments Lew didn't know how to react. He glanced at Charlie Huntz, at Jed Clancy, at the nearest of those with whom he'd recently played poker. All expressions were grim, as though they expected a burst of violence that would lead to someone's death. Fearlessly, Lew had faced a man with a gun on several occasions but now, for the first time, he felt a damp line of sweat forming on his upper lip. As the dark eyes of the man in buckskin stared at him with undisguised hatred, he felt the cold grip of uncertainty in his stomach.

He looked at the cavalry captain and thought he saw in his face a flicker of decision: that being an officer he ought to demonstrate his authority and prevent violence. A second ticked by, two, then the silence was broken from an unexpected quarter. The voice was slurred but the words were distinct.

'I've got an Indian wife, too, and that man' — everyone in the room was looking at the drunk who had been slumped over the table and whose right arm now pointed in accusatory fashion at Wes Gray — 'is the one I blame.'

5

Wes Gray's accuser was unkempt, his features not only grubby and shadowed with bristles but ruddied by too much whiskey. The alcohol was also responsible for the unsteady, watery look in his eyes. His dark hair stuck out in irregular fashion which, despite his inebriated condition, gave him a somewhat boyish appearance that somehow softened the gruffness of his comment. Despite the man's sullen appearance and manner Wes had no difficulty in recognizing Jim Taylor, whose homestead he'd planned to visit before rejoining the wagon train.

★   ★   ★

The men had met three years earlier when Jim Taylor and his new wife, Alice, had been part of the wagon train

75

being led to Oregon by Caleb Dodge. Unlike his current practice of not meeting the wagons until they were due to cross the Blue, Wes, at that time, travelled with the wagons all the way from Independence. So he became a familiar figure to the emigrants and struck up an acquaintance with Jim and Alice, which included taking evening meals with them when his duties permitted.

Then, somewhere between the Blue and the Platte river crossings, disaster struck. Walking at the side of their ox-drawn wagon, Alice's dress got caught up in a wheel and she was dragged under in an instant. Even though the pace of the wagons was no greater than three miles an hour it wasn't easy to stop the team. Alice was crushed and died where she lay.

Two days later, to distract Jim from the loss of his wife, Wes took him hunting. They rode far, to the valley of Mildwater Creek, and the first moment he looked upon it Jim decided to travel no further westward. Wes didn't discourage him for he himself had often looked upon this valley with the thought that it was where he would choose to settle when the urge to wander the West had left him.

However there were drawbacks to living here, which he didn't keep from Jim. First there was the dangers of isolation. Not only was the simplest accident a risk to life when there was no one else around to help, but the lack of someone else to talk to had been known to send tough old mountain men crazy. Then there was the vagaries of the weather: the summers were hot and the winters bitterly cold. Through it all he would have to work the land and tend his stock just to survive. Jim was not to be deterred. Next day he pulled his wagon and livestock from the line and settled in the V-shaped piece of land where the Mildwater Creek meets the South Platte River.

Alone he worked, ploughing and planting his crop. He built his cabin, corralled his horses and put his milk cows to pasture. For weeks at a stretch he saw no one. Occasionally an army patrol arrived bringing news of events outside his valley, especially when there were rumours of unrest among the Indians. Sometimes bands of curious Sioux watched him from the hills. They didn't interfere with him but their presence worried him. When Wes next visited the valley he tried to solve Jim's problem.

'They're your neighbours,' he told him. 'Go and visit them. Make friends. Choose a wife.'

'A wife?'

'Sure. Marry one of their women and they'll know you mean them no harm. Learn their language. Understand their ways. Her family'll come a-visiting from time to time. It'll be company for you.'

It was a proposition that Jim found difficult to accept. Lingering thoughts of Alice formed a barrier against remarrying, but his major problem was an inability to grasp the notion that a village of tribesmen were his neighbours, not his enemies. None the less, Wes took him to a nearby village of Ogallalah Sioux.

There was little risk in such a visit; two men weren't any sort of threat to an entire village, besides which Wes knew that the Sioux were as curious about the ways of the white people as the whites were of theirs. Of course, when they got to within a mile of the village a band of braves encircled them shouting threats and war-whoops, but it was merely a demonstration, a means of showing their own bravery while testing that of their visitors. Wes told Jim to sit still.

'They'll be looking to count coup by touching us with their sticks.'

As if he'd been waiting for the explanation a young buck urged his horse forward and ranged alongside Wes. He swung his feathered stick at Wes's shoulder but the scout wasn't prepared to suffer such ignominy. Strictly speaking, counting coup only occurred in battle, a product of the inter-tribal wars. It was a means of showing a warrior's bravery by touching an armed enemy with nothing more than a stick. The arrival of the white man's gun had changed the rule. To show disdain for the weapon that avoided the need for hand-to-hand fighting, it was permitted to touch any armed American, a practice that the white people found undignified if not downright frightening.

At the last moment Wes ducked under the stick, getting low enough to reach down to grab the Indian's foot. With a quick movement he heaved him over the side of his horse. No Indian likes to be unhorsed but Wes wasn't looking to embarrass anyone; just the opposite: he was hoping to make friends. So, as the Indian fell from his horse, Wes allowed himself to fall to the ground too, in such a manner that the other Indians thought his clumsiness was the cause of both men being dumped in the dust.

To emphasize his own humiliation Wes filled his hands with dirt and threw it in the air so that it came down over his own head.

'A-Hey,' shouted Wes, and laughed. His action was something of a gamble, but not one where the odds were stacked against him. If the mood of the group had been warlike their reception would have been much more hostile. From his experience with other tribes of Plains Indians, he knew that, other than tales of bravery in battle, there was nothing that Indians liked better than a campfire story that would make the elders laugh. Everything depended on the reaction of the Sioux braves.

At first there was nothing but silence and Wes wondered if he had misread the situation. Then one of the mounted braves laughed and soon they were all laughing. All except the one who had been unseated, who knew the truth of the matter. Still smiling, Wes looked at him under the bodies of their horses. After a moment the unseated warrior grinned, filled his hands with dirt and threw it over his own head.

Wes got to his feet and withdrew the Arapaho pipe that he carried in his saddle-bag. Mingling the few words of Sioux he knew with the universal sign language of the Plains tribes, he told them that their kinsmen, the Arapaho, called him brother and knew him by the name Medicine Feather. He had come, he told them, to smoke with the brave warriors of the Sioux.

The name Medicine Feather was not unknown to them, nor was the fact that he had travelled with 'Blanket' Jim Bridger. With some ceremony Jim Taylor and Wes were escorted into their village.

It was a small village of less than forty lodges, which spread a quarter of a mile along the same stream of water that eventually ran down to the Mildwater valley. It was a warm day and the skins were rolled up from the bottom of the lodges to let air circulate. Here and there men lay on the ground enjoying the warmth of the day and watching the women at work. Others tended their horses or sat cross-legged in conversation with their friends. All of them stood when they saw the approaching group with the white men in the middle.

Wes and Jim first saw Sky as they made their way to the lodge of the chief, Kicking Bear. She was stretching hide with three other girls and her big brown eyes watched them with an interest that was deeper than mere curiosity. Her shy smile illuminated a keenness for knowledge. From the interest their visit had generated Wes suspected they were the first white men to visit this village, which could mean that they were the first *wasicun* (white people) Sky had seen. She wore a doeskin dress decorated with buffalo hair and small coloured stones. The unadorned moccasins on her feet were made of the same material. Her long black hair was greased and plaited in the general style. She had high cheekbones, a straight, proud bearing, and was as slender and as graceful as a fawn. Her eyes followed them to the very entrance of Kicking Bear's tepee. Wes noted how Jim returned the look.

News of their approach had been sent on ahead to Kicking Bear and he greeted them adorned with a headdress of eagle feathers that reached to his ankles, a display designed to impress the visitors and to advertise to his own people that he was welcoming them with honour.

'*Hohahe,*' he began, which Wes knew was a greeting of welcome, telling them he was glad they had come. In a little speech from which Wes identified the words *wasicun* and Lakota it was clear that Kicking Bear was voicing a desire for Americans and Sioux to be friends. Five men formed a line beside Kicking Bear; older men, the village council, gathered around silently, heads held high, blankets folded over their arms as though an emblem of their position in the tribe. They sat in a circle outside

Kicking Bear's tepee and a pipe was passed around.

Wes told the gathered Sioux that he and Jim had come in friendship. They had recognized Jim as the man living alone by the creek which, in the ways of the Lakota, was a bad thing. He needed a wife. He should choose one from the girls of Kicking Bear's village. It was clear to Wes that Jim had already made his choice. His eyes had continually strayed to where the girl with the big brown eyes worked tirelessly at the deerskin.

'Her name is Apo Hopa,' Wes told Jim after making enquiries, 'which roughly translates into Beautiful Dawn.'

'Like a pink sky,' said Jim.

'That's just a part of it,' Wes told him. 'Her name captures all the good things of a new day. The first birdsong; the fragrance of the forest; the sun warming the earth beneath bare feet. All the sights and sounds and smells that please and carry a promise of pleasure. Her birth must have been regarded as the start of something new and good for her family.'

When Jim and Apo Hopa married a few weeks later Wes was not present. He'd moved on, keeping his appointment at the Blue with the new train of migrants. The wedding wasn't much of a ceremony, nothing more than the presentation of a gift to Grey Moccasin, Sky's father, which consisted of a couple of store-bought blankets and a pot or two. Then Apo Hopa clambered up behind Jim and he headed his horse back home. No doubt Grey Moccasin could have got more if his daughter had chosen someone from the tribe, but having a daughter married to a white man raised his importance to a degree that ten horses couldn't equal.

The Sioux weren't opposed to sharing the land with white settlers, they were opposed to being told that they could no longer hunt or live or travel on land that had been open to them for generations. They were in awe of the machinery and weapons that the white people brought and were happy to deal with any white people who were prepared to share their possessions and obtain goods for them. Grey Moccasin, no doubt, regarded Jim Taylor as an unending source of white man's goods.

It was another year before Wes visited again. From the ridge where he'd first shown Jim the valley he could see all the work that had been undertaken. Crops were growing, another shed had been built and yet another was in the process of being built. He could see Jim at work on the building as he rode down to the cabin. When he was within hailing distance he gave a shout and waved his hat so that even if Jim hadn't yet recognized him he would know it was someone with peaceable intentions. Even so, when he reached the rail that designated his yard from open range, Jim grabbed his rifle and held it in a threatening manner.

Apo Hopa was a step behind, her right arm outstretched to rest on Jim's left, signifying that the gun wasn't necessary. Wes had seen her only once yet she'd recognized him long before Jim had. She raised her face to Wes and again he was struck by the grace of her movement and the allure of shyness in her big brown eyes. Looking at her gave him pleasure and he thought she should have been called *Tacicala*, which is Fawn.

If Apo Hopa's face displayed pleasure at Wes's arrival, Jim Taylor's showed only wariness. Even when he recognized the scout it took several seconds before his finger moved from inside the trigger guard. Wes raised his open hand, showing his palm to Jim and Apo Hopa, and said '*Hau*,' before stepping down from the saddle.

'Fee?' Apo Hopa gestured towards the house after the first greetings had been exchanged.

'She means coffee,' said Jim. 'Goddammit, been here a year and all she can manage is half a word.'

'So you're fluent in Sioux?' Wes expected a grin or a chuckle in response but Jim's jaw remained tight, unappreciative of the scout's humour.

'All I get is 'fee' or signs and grunts.'

'Well you both look well on it.' Wes spoke a few words in the Lakota tongue to Apo Hopa. She smiled and giggled and turned back to the house to get the coffee.

'What did you say to her?' Jim asked, his eyes dark with blunt suspicion.

Wes wasn't able to provide a true interpretation, it was a phrase he'd picked up from Jim Bridger, something he used when he wanted to say something nice to a Sioux girl. Of course acting blindly on something Blanket Jim told him could prove dangerous, he being an inveterate practical joker, but so far it hadn't landed Wes in any trouble.

'Just told her she looked very pretty. You don't object, do you?'

Whether he did or not wasn't clear. Jim's answer was nothing more than a grunt as he, too, turned towards the house. Over dinner Wes learned about their winter hardships. For five weeks the snow had been so deep that they hadn't been able to leave the cabin. They'd lost one of their cows and a horse. The horse had died in the shed he'd built for the livestock, but the cow had disappeared before he'd got them rounded up.

'Indians,' Jim Taylor said. 'Probably killed it and ate it while we were freezing in this cabin.'

Wes didn't want to argue with him but his words were out without any thought of offending him.

'If you were huddled up against the cold they would be too.'

'Huh. Cold don't bother them. They are used to it.'

Wes knew that that was nonsense. He'd wintered in Indian villages and knew that there was little they could do but survive. He threw in some logic.

'If the snow was too deep for you then it had to be too deep for them, too.'

Jim shook his head. 'I don't know

how they do it but they can move about wherever and whenever they want to.'

Again, Wes tried to put some humour in his answer.

'Then you should get Apo Hopa to show you how it's done.' Wes looked across at her. He figured she would know by the tone of their voices that they couldn't agree about something and, by the way she dropped her look from his, Wes was sure she knew that it involved her people.

Jim Taylor cast a long, puzzled glance in his wife's direction, as though Wes had said something too deep for his understanding. Eventually he spoke, his words delivered with a gruff solemnity which was meant to carry the conviction that his livestock had ended up in Sioux bellies.

'Cow never even turned up in spring when the thaw came.'

'Wolves,' declared Wes. 'Wolves would have got it.'

'Sioux,' said Jim. 'Thievin' Sioux. Well if they come around here trying to steal anything else they won't all get home again.' He threw a meaningful look at Apo Hopa but she didn't raise her head. Wes figured she'd heard him rant on the subject before and that, even if she didn't know the words, she understood his meaning well enough. His only reason for visiting had been to bring some friendly company but it didn't seem to be working.

After they'd eaten Wes offered to lend a hand with the chores. Sullenly, as though suspicious of Wes's motive for helping, Jim declined. None the less, when Jim went to the barn, Wes stepped into the yard and set about splitting logs for kindling. He hadn't been at it long when he heard his name called and from the shadow of the barn door Jim beckoned. They climbed into the hay loft from where, lying flat, they looked out of the open loft doors. The land to the north rose to a wooded ridge and for a several moments they gazed at it without speaking.

'Do you see them?' Jim asked.

Wes did. Six Sioux braves, not attempting to hide, looking down on the homestead.

'Ogallalah,' said Wes.

'They want Sky,' said Jim.

'Sky?' Then Wes realized he was talking about Apo Hopa. He recalled the day he'd interpreted Apo Hopa's name and how Jim had likened it to a pink sky. Sky, it seemed, had stuck in Jim's mind. He spoke it now as if it was her true name. He doubted if Jim had ever used her Sioux name. Probably didn't remember it, and it was a clear fact that he had made no effort to become friends with her people.

Jim spoke again, keeping his voice low as though anything higher than a whisper would carry to the warriors on the distant ridge.

'The one on the pinto. He's the one who's after her. Always up there.'

The Indian described by Jim Taylor was at the front of the group. He had a strong, athletic body. The tops of eagle feathers showed above his black hair, which hung loose to his shoulders.

'Don't they come down to the house?' Wes asked. Jim turned his head sharply, his eyes wide.

'They'll kill me if I let them get near the house. Kill me and take Sky.'

'They're not looking for trouble,' Wes said. 'No paint. If they haven't painted their faces they're not looking to fight.' It was clear that Jim didn't agree.

Wes was worried by Jim's behaviour, worried that the loneliness of the life he'd chosen was akin to the cabin fever that affected the old fur trappers. His concern stretched to Apo Hopa's safety, although he had seen no sign of mistreatment by her husband. Even so, it was clear to Wes that the strain of a solitary life had affected Jim's reason. Although unfounded, his distrust of the Sioux had begun to control his life and distort his thinking.

When the party of Sioux rode away Wes, too, prepared to leave. It was in his mind to talk to Sky, try to learn more about Jim's behaviour both towards herself and towards visitors to the homestead, but the opportunity never arose. Jim, seemingly as suspicious of Wes's intentions towards Sky as of those of the Sioux on the ridge, made sure they were never alone. However, on a couple of occasions Wes caught Sky watching him in that way she had, that mixture of acceptance yet seeking knowledge; of shyness yet knowing all.

When he left them she filled his canteen at the water pump by the trough. The tips of her fingers brushed the back of his hand as she handed it to him. Perhaps it had been accidental. He hadn't been back to find out.

★ ★ ★

Now, as everyone turned to listen to him, Jim's drunken utterance dissipated the tension that had grown between Wes Gray and Lew Butler.

'Sioux. You can't trust them. They're just waiting for an opportunity.'

Captain O'Malley crossed the room

to the table which Jim Taylor still slouched over.

'An opportunity for what?'

Jim looked up at him, squinted as though trying to focus on the officer's face and said,

'Attack.'

'What do you know, Jim?' Wes asked. 'Have you had some trouble?'

'They watch me. All the time. They're up in the hills watching.'

'Why? What do they want?'

Jim laughed, a bitter sound. He refreshed the contents of the shot glass with more from the bottle and threw it all down his throat. His eyes held a look that wasn't just affected by whiskey.

'Sky,' he said. 'One of them wants her and means to kill me to get her.'

Wes was beset by two emotions. The first was concern for Jim Taylor. He was disturbed by the change in him. He was haggard, his skin grey-coloured, his cheeks empty and slack, further evidence of the loneliness fever he'd witnessed the last time they'd met. The other feeling he had was one of exasperation. What he knew about the Sioux made the truth of Jim's last words unlikely. In Sioux society it was the woman who chose the man. If she wasn't happy with the one she chose she could leave him and pick another. There were no recriminations. The husband had to let her go. It was a sign of weakness to try to hang on to an unwilling wife. So, if Sky preferred another man she would have gone to him. Jim Taylor's head dropped on to the table again.

'He's talking nonsense,' Wes told Captain O'Malley.

'Who is this man?' asked O'Malley.

'A homesteader. His spread is across on the South Platte.'

'Deep in Sioux country?'

Wes nodded agreement.

'Then his information is vital. If he says the Sioux are on the move we must believe him.'

'He didn't say the Sioux were on the move.'

'He said they were in the hills.'

'The Sioux are always in the hills. They are hunters and most of what they hunt lives in the hills. Jed,' Wes turned his attention to the storekeeper and indicated the sleeping figure of Jim Taylor, 'how long has he been like this?'

'Came in this morning, bought some supplies and loaded his wagon. Then set to with the bottle. He's been drinking ever since.'

'Does this happen regular?'

'Does now. When he first started turning up here he used to be in, loaded and out again with little fuss. Then he began hanging around, supposedly hoping to hear news about the Indian situation. But it soon became apparent that he just wanted to hit the bottle. Hardly converses with anyone. Like he's afraid to let people know his business. Sometimes he stays here overnight. Well, you can see why.'

'Does he come often?'

'Usually once a month. Soldiers have taken to calling him the Squaw Man.'

He cast a wary look at Wes lest he'd taken offence, offered a defensive kind of shrug and hurried to explain.

'They reckon he's gone mad. Won't let them dismount when they call by his place. Orders his woman into the shack and won't let her out 'til they've gone. Just stands there holding his rifle while the officer passes on any news or gossip as he sees fit.'

'Comes in here alone?'

'Sure. Never brings the Indian woman with him.' He looked at the untidy bundle that was Jim Taylor. 'I'll get a bucket of water. That's usually what it takes to revive him.'

Curly Clayport pushed his way through the batwing doors.

'Shouldn't you be heading north, Captain? Colonel Flint ordered you to find out what happened to the stage-coach.'

'I know my duty, Mr Clayport. As it happens we're just about to leave. Mr Gray, are you coming with us?'

Wes nodded. As he passed the table

where Lew Butler and Charlie Huntz sat, he stopped. 'I ain't forgetting what you said. If I hear you insult my wife or her people again I'll kill you.'

Supposing them not to be above shooting him in the back he backed out through the batwing doors and climbed up on to Red.

Clara Clancy, Jed's wife, spoke to Lew and Charlie.

'You picked the wrong man to upset. They say he knows more ways of killing a man than all the tribes from Chicago to the Alamo. Still, he's gone now. He'll find the missing coach. He's the best tracker this side of the Missouri and all the best trackers *are* this side of the Missouri.'

'Who is he?' Charlie asked.

'His name. Why, that's Wes Gray. Didn't you know?'

'Wes Gray,' Charlie repeated softly.

He and Lew Butler exchanged worried looks.

6

It was late afternoon when the patrol found the deserted stagecoach, its doors open and its skittish horses trying hard to chew grass and leaves despite the handicap of bridles, harness and the inability to separate themselves from each other. Captain O'Malley ordered two troopers to unharness the beasts from the coach and tend to them while the rest of the party searched for the driver and the shotgun guard.

The six-horse team hadn't wandered far from the scene of the hold-up and it required only a brief inspection of the bodies of Ben Garland and Jake Welchman to prove that they hadn't been killed by Indians. The busted strongbox was evidence enough that robbers had waylaid the coach. Wes dismounted and checked around for signs.

'There are signs of a scuffle here,' he told the officer, 'and I think there was a woman involved.'

'A woman?' echoed O'Malley. Wes drew O'Malley's attention to some smaller footprints.

'Whoever made those was a lot lighter than everyone else.'

'Could it be a boy?'

Wes studied them closely, noted the shape and style of the heelprint.

'I don't think so.' Then, to prove his conclusion wasn't based on one clue alone, he pointed across the trail. 'Over here.'

He moved forward and indicated an area at the side of the trail.

'Looks as though the scuffle ended up on the ground here, and judging by the area that's been disturbed I'd say the one on his back was wearing a dress. That being the case I'd suggest she was a passenger.' He looked at O'Malley and grinned. 'I've heard of female bandits before but I've never heard of one holding up a stagecoach wearing a dress.'

'Sergeant,' Captain O'Malley shouted. 'See if there's any luggage under the flap.' He spoke next to Wes Gray. 'I have no orders to pursue anybody,' he said. 'That's a job for the local law officer, or Wells Fargo themselves. Let's get these bodies into the stagecoach. When the horses are rested we'll return to the fort.'

'Sir,' called the sergeant, 'there are some trunks here.'

While O'Malley investigated the luggage Wes gave the area a thorough examination. He found hoof-prints where the outlaws had waited in ambush and also signs of their departure over the high bluffs. When he'd done he returned to the coach to find the captain in a state of great agitation. One of the trunks was open and O'Malley held two small framed photographs.

'We must find her,' he said to the sergeant. 'Mount up and scour the hills.'

The captain's sudden decision surprised the sergeant.

'Sir?' His single word conveyed the sense that the order was improper.

'Are you questioning me, Sergeant?'

Seeking a good cause that would justify his apparent reluctance to obey a command the sergeant said:

'There aren't enough of us, sir. We can't go in different directions, anyone who came across the robbers would be sure to be outnumbered. Like you told Mr Gray, it's not our job.'

O'Malley's anger flared. 'I'll decide what is our job.'

Wes Gray, confused by the captain's agitation, asked for an explanation.

'The girl,' said O'Malley. 'It's Ellie. Ellie Rogers. My fiancée.' He handed Wes the photographs. One showed the head and shoulders of a smiling young girl. The other was a photograph of O'Malley himself. 'I've got to find her.'

'No,' said Wes. 'You've got to get back to Laramie and defuse the rumours of a Sioux uprising.'

'I can't abandon Ellie.' Then, almost as though he were talking to himself, he added, 'What on earth was she doing here.' In distracted fashion, the young officer peered inside the coach, almost as though he expected to see Ellie sitting in a corner, her presence overlooked by the sergeant who had reached the vehicle first.

He turned away, his face red with anger. Then he slapped his gloves on the palm of his hand as if he'd arrived at an important decision. He strode towards his horse, placed a hand on the saddle, raised a foot to the stirrup. Then he paused. His desire to pursue the men who had kidnapped his fiancée was obvious to every man present.

From his reconnaissance of the scene Wes had detected that three men were involved in the robbery. He also knew that one had ridden away carrying extra weight. It didn't take much detective work to assume that that additional burden had been Ellie. He had found the line of their departure, eastwards, towards the North Platte, and he was anxious to start after them knowing that once they reached and crossed that river it would be difficult for anyone to track them.

That, however, was information he chose to keep from Captain O'Malley. Instead, he pointed in the direction in which the robbers had gone and used the minimum of words to describe his intentions before climbing into the saddle.

'There are three of them, riding that way. They are already a day ahead. I'll travel faster alone. I'll do what I can to bring her back.'

Reluctant to leave the task of finding Ellie to another, Captain O'Malley stepped forward to grab at Red's bridle. The sergeant moved more quickly, putting himself between the officer and the horse. He held O'Malley's angry glare, knowing that his action might be interpreted as insubordination. But the look in his eyes was one of sympathy, as though he was telling the captain that he understood his distress, that he would want to react in the same way, but would also want a good friend to stop him and guide him to do his duty.

'It's for the best, sir,' he said, keeping his voice low so that his words didn't carry to the rest of the troopers. 'Wes Gray can follow tracks better than most Indians. If your lady can be brought back he's the one to do it.'

Without waiting for further orders he set about supervising the men in preparation for the journey back to Fort Laramie.

* * *

For Wes Gray the trail was easy to follow. The flattened path where the grass had been broken down by galloping horses was clear to see on the rising ground. The robbers, it seemed, were disdainful of pursuit. Either they believed that the telltale signs of their passing would have disappeared before any posse could be put into the field, or they were confident that they would be untraceable once they reached the numerous valleys and streams that ran down to the North Platte.

He'd covered little more than a mile when he pulled Red into a walk and ambled a few strides off the trail. A mild breeze was blowing, shifting the leaves of the trees, the grass on the hillside and the slender branches of the ground shrubs. In one of the shrubs something else moved. Wes knew by its colour that it was man-made. He hung low in the saddle and scooped the object free of the fronds on which it was snagged. It was an old, grey hat that had gone soft with age. Wes examined it but it had no identifying marks. He tucked it under the tie strings of his blanket roll to stop it blowing away and tapped his heels against Red's flanks, instructing him to pick up speed again.

An hour later he dismounted to rest Red and to check the tracks he was following. For a while now he had seen the imprints of one horse become more pronounced, proof that the one carrying double was tiring in its effort to keep up with the others. Shadows were lengthening and the heat of the day was beginning to diminish. Wes checked the eastern horizon and decided he had little more than an hour of daylight left. He could clearly see the direction the robbers had taken; a path of beaten-down grass disappeared around the side of a hillock.

'Come on, boy,' he said to the horse as he clambered back on board, 'let's get as far as we can tonight.' With an obvious trail to follow, he pushed Red hard.

As dusk approached they breasted a ridge that looked down on a broad stream. The tracks he was trailing were still discernible but Wes knew that if the robbers had taken the precaution of riding a little way along in the water, only time and luck would permit him to find them again. He drew his rifle and slowly rode down to the water's edge. This, he knew, was a good place to camp for the night but it paid to advance carefully: someone else might have the same idea.

He saw the body on the grassy slope. Two arrows protruded from its back, their shafts snapped off and discarded. Peering round, Wes checked for movement in the surrounding bushes. All was still. Nightjars sang and fluttered somewhere near. A good sign. Wes climbed down from his horse and approached the dead man.

The body had been stripped, scalped and mutilated. He collected the broken arrow shafts and examined them. There was no mistaking their origin. Shoshone. Making the most of the diminishing light he tried to piece together what had happened. The three riders he was pursuing had stopped here, then had been attacked by Shoshones. Unshod ponies had come across the river. There had been an exchange of fire, a fact indicated by the spent shells that were scattered on the ground a short distance from the body.

If any Indians had been killed it seemed logical to assume that their comrades had been back to collect the bodies. Two shod and several unshod horses had gone back up the bank. The likelihood was that two of the robbers had survived the initial charge and made a break for freedom pursued by the Shoshone. The question that bothered Wes was: what had happened to the girl?

Near the body he found a rawhide strip which was knotted in the middle but had been cut with a sharp blade. Wes surmised it had been used to bind something, possibly the girl's hands, but there was no other sign of her. What, he wondered, had happened to her after the attack? Had she escaped and wandered away and was now lost in the hills? Or had the Shoshone taken her? A white woman was a prize worth capturing, a slave to take back to the village, a creature to perform every menial task the womenfolk demanded. But if the Shoshone had taken her, why cut away her bindings?

Wes re-examined the body. Without clothes there was no way of knowing the man's identity. He gazed at the face. There was something familiar about it but Wes knew he had never seen it before. Wes had no means by which to transport the body back to civilization for a proper burial, nor the inclination to return to Laramie until he'd searched longer for the girl. Travelling light, he was devoid of a suitable tool with which to dig a grave, so he set about gathering rocks to pile on top of the corpse. This was the best he could do to prevent it being devoured by carrion-eating birds and scavenging animals. As he was lifting rocks from the river bed he suddenly realized that he was not alone.

They were Sioux. Six of them, motionless astride motionless ponies. Their faces were painted, half-red, half-black, with a broad band of yellow crossing each face from cheek to cheek. War paint. Wes placed the last rock on the mound he had made over the body, then removed his hat and wiped his sleeve over his brow. When he had replaced his hat he held up his hand in the traditional greeting sign and began to walk towards the group. If they were here to make war against him they would have killed him before he had known they were there. One of them, a muscular brave astride a brown piebald pony, moved slowly forward to meet him. There was something familiar about the brave, something familiar in the way he sat his horse, but the paint on his face made his features difficult to recognize. Using a mix of Sioux words, Arapaho words and sign language Wes held a conversation with him.

'I am Medicine Feather, brother of the Arapaho.'

'*Wiyaka Wakan* is known to the people of the Ogallalah.'

'I'm looking for a white woman who was taken from a coach by bad men. She was here when the white men fought Shoshone raiders.'

'We are hunting Shoshone. Last night they raided our village and stole ponies. Kicking Bear, our chief, was killed.'

Wes was saddened by the news. Kicking Bear had always stood against war with the white men and a new chief might lead his village in a different direction.

'I have smoked a pipe with Kicking Bear,' Wes said. 'He was a great man.'

The Indian nodded.

Wes asked, 'Who is now chief of the Ogallalah?'

'*Mila Luhtah*, Red Knife, who is young and wise.'

'I hope he leads his people in the way of peace.'

'There will never be peace with the Shoshone. They are dogs. When we catch them we will kill them.'

An idea flashed into the scout's mind. If he rode with these Sioux warriors he might be able to rescue Ellie Rogers when they caught up with the Shoshones. He told the Sioux brave what he had seen the previous day.

'The Shoshones split into two groups in the Valley Where Two Waters Fall. Perhaps they plan to meet there before returning to their own country.'

'A-hey,' yelled the warrior. 'It is good. If we ride hard we can catch them.'

'I wish to ride with you,' said Wes. 'As you want your ponies so I want the woman I seek.'

Then the Sioux brave surprised him.

'The Shoshone do not have the woman,' he said.

'How do you know? Where is she?' Wes feared the brave's words meant that Ellie was dead, that her discarded body had been discovered by some tribespeople. He was astonished by the response.

'The Shoshone do not have the woman. We saw her when she was a prisoner of some white men. One had hair on his face the colour of your horse. Later we heard the sounds of fighting and we found her here alone. I took her to the lodge of my sister. She is well.'

'Your sister?'

'You know her. She is the squaw of your friend.'

'Apo Hopa! Apo Hopa is your sister?' Wes recalled the day he had watched the band of Sioux from the hayloft of Jim Taylor's barn. This was the brave whom Jim suspected of trying to lure Sky away. He was her brother, watching over her to see that she was well.

'Yes, I am her brother.' He continued speaking and his next words held another surprise for Wes.

'We have met before, Medicine Feather. You and I have smoked a pipe together.'

Wes looked closely at him; his features were typical of the Sioux people but perhaps there was something about the shape of his eyes that made him think he should remember the brave.

Lightly, the Indian sprang from his pony and squatted beside Wes.

'A-hey,' he said. He filled his hands with dust and threw it up so that it came down over his head.'

Wes grinned and followed suit.

'A-hey,' he said. He heard the laughter of the other warriors who had remained further up the hillside.

'You gave me my name,' Sky's brother told Wes. 'Now I am called Throws The Dust.'

After the Sioux had ridden away and with darkness fast approaching, Wes decided to make camp for the night. Even though he was sure the Shoshones were not close by, he chose to camp without a fire. There was a suitable spot halfway between the river and the ridge, sheltered and secluded among a clutch of pines. He picketed Red close by and fed him oats and water from his hat before chewing a chunk of jerked beef for his own supper.

As he spread out his bedroll he heard the rustle in the trees. Red had picked up the sound a moment earlier, giving a little warning snicker to the scout. Wes drew his six-gun and pressed himself against a tree, silently watching and listening.

Another movement sounded, this time more distinct. Wes discounted Indians; they wouldn't be so clumsy. Again a noise, louder this time, and he wished he'd picked up his rifle. Perhaps it was a grizzly bear: this was their domain. But he knew Red would have been spooked if it were a grizzly. Instead he was standing calmly, unconcerned by whatever or whoever was approaching.

There came a final crackle of twigs underfoot and a scratching of leaves and branches, and a dun-coloured horse emerged from the deeper reaches of the little wood. It was saddled but riderless and it stopped, shyly, when it saw Red. Wes left his hiding-place, reholstered his gun and took hold of its bridle. The horse was trembling from withers to hindquarters.

'Tired and hungry, are you?' Wes spoke gently. 'I guess that was your owner I've just finished burying.' He unsaddled the horse and ground-tied him beside Red before feeding him with oats and water. 'Perhaps something in these saddle-bags will tell us the name of that fella.'

There wasn't much in the saddle-bags: some items of clothing, ammunition, a harmonica and a leather billfold. Wes checked its contents; there were a handful of dollar notes and a single folded document. The document declared that the bearer, Clement Jonson Butler, had on the twenty-third day of September, 1865, renounced the Confederate Army and sworn an Oath of Allegiance to the United States of America. It was his end-of-war discharge paper.

* * *

The next morning, knowing that Ellie Rogers was safe, Wes followed the trail of the fleeing robbers. With the reins of Clem Butler's horse fastened to his saddle horn, he soon came across the long-grass battle scene marked by the scavenger-scarred body of a dead saddle horse. Wes dismounted, removed his hat and scratched his head. He studied the signs of battle and, other than the fact that it had begun at the river, everything up to the defeat of the Indians coincided with the story related by the two men who had reached Laramie. Which, if they were the men who had been involved in this fight, meant that they were also the men who had robbed the stage, murdered the driver and guard and kidnapped Ellie Rogers.

However, they had claimed that both of their horses were killed in the battle; whereas before him was distinct evidence that one of the horses had left the scene unharmed. The men had also ridden into Laramie on Sioux ponies, yet all the evidence here pointed to a Shoshone war party. Even without Throws The Dust's testimony Wes knew that Shoshone and Sioux would never fight side by side.

So had there been two similar battles with two white men winning out against a superior number of Indians? It seemed unlikely, and if the survivors of this battle weren't the two men in Laramie where were they now? What was clear to Wes was that they hadn't gone back to help Clement Jonson Butler or Ellie Rogers. Perhaps they'd considered them dead before they'd made a run for it. Wes pulled the arrow from the belly of the dead horse and wrapped it inside the grey hat. This arrow, too, was Shoshone, evidence that the Sioux had not been involved in the fight.

Wes decided not to fetch Ellie Rogers from Jim Taylor's cabin. He was content to report her situation to the army. Colonel Flint, no doubt, would dispatch Captain O'Malley to the Mildwater Valley homestead for a reunion with his girl. Instead, he followed the trail of the single horse, considering it his duty to track down the remaining robbers even though he knew that Caleb Dodge would soon require him to help with the crossing at the Platte River. Not only were they robbers, but killers and kidnappers, too.

He came across the second dead horse with its broken leg and bullet in the brain as he neared the end of the long-grass country. His suspicion that the two men in Laramie were the men he was following hardened; those suspicions were occupying his thoughts as he entered the rolling hill land that led back to Laramie.

* * *

Lew Butler and Charlie Huntz sat alone in Clancy's store eating steaks that Clara had set before them free of charge; reward for 'two brave Indian fighters who are making the West a safer place to live'. To their ears, those words were more welcome than her earlier declaration that the man they'd antagonized was Wes Gray, especially after the return of the cavalry patrol with the news that the scout had gone in search of the captain's kidnapped fiancée.

'That's the one they call Medicine Feather,' Charlie Huntz had said, keeping his voice low lest it should betray his nervousness.

Lew was thinking of their carelessness after the robbery. They had done nothing to hide their tracks, thinking they would lose any pursuers at the North Platte or when they struck a well-used trail. But Clem and his lust had changed all that. Even if he was only half as good as his reputation, Wes Gray would have no difficulty in following the trail of the robbers back to Laramie. He would find Clem's body and one look at his face would be enough to identify him as his brother. Then he would find the spot where Charlie and he had fought the Indians, followed by the dead horse. Then there were those two Indian boys, the last sign on the way into Laramie.

'One of two things we can do, Charlie. Either we clear out of here before the squaw man gets here, or we go and meet him.'

'What do you suggest, Lew?' asked Charlie, with his usual dependence on Lew's thinking, Lew chewed on his last piece of steak before answering.

'It'll look suspicious if we pull out before nightfall, but Gray might be back here before sundown. If we leave now we might not get far enough ahead to lose him. So, I reckon we go and meet him. Stop him from pointing the finger at us. Then we stay here one more night and head south again to spend some money.'

He picked up his hat, admired its silver discs and put it on his head. 'Come on,' he said. 'We need to purchase some horses.'

★   ★   ★

They chose a spot that gave them a commanding view of a valley down which they knew Wes Gray must ride. They had been there since early morning, rifles ready, horses close by for a speedy escape. They had been there so long they were beginning to wonder if he'd chosen another route. Charlie Huntz was edgy.

'Should I ride up ahead? See if I can see him?'

'Don't be stupid, Charlie. He has to come this way.'

No sooner had the words left Lew's mouth than the two men saw him in the distance, close to the mouth of the narrow valley.

'That's Clem's horse he's leading,' said Lew. 'He's sure to know we were with him.

Charlie raised his rifle but Lew advised patience.

'Wait until you're absolutely sure. He can get a lot closer yet. We'll fire together. He won't get up again with two bullets in him.'

They lay on their stomachs and sighted along the long barrels of their Winchesters.

'Ready? Lew asked.

'Yep,' said Charlie.

'On three. One . . . two . . . '

Before Lew reached three a rifle shot exploded somewhere down the valley. Arms flung wide, Wes Gray fell from his horse, an unmoving form in the long grass. Lew and Charlie eased the pressure from their triggers and looked at each other. Suddenly, a band of Indians emerged from the folds of the hills and descended on the felled scout. They surrounded him, one of them sitting astride his chest, scalping knife glinting in the bright morning sun.

'Well, well,' said Charlie. 'Looks like we've been saved a job.'

Lew grinned. 'Let's get out of here.

7

Hearing was the first of Wes's senses to return as he lay on the ground, but it was his instinct for survival that latched on to those pinpricks of sound and guided his mind through the confusing black void to the light which lay beyond. How long that journey to consciousness took he could not have said. Perhaps mere moments, perhaps much longer, but as he neared the end of his struggle he recognized the noise as voices which were neither clear nor friendly.

Suddenly all his senses kicked in. A shriek was uttered, so close to his face that he felt a spray of spittle. This was accompanied by the foul smell of stale animal grease. Pain followed, his head engulfed by a continuous, throbbing ache. He kept his eyes closed, aware that excess light would increase the pain and pain was an enemy that had to be overcome if he was to arrange his thoughts in some sort of order. But there was no relief for him. A long, piercing shaft of pain, an intense white void of agony, lanced from the top of his head to some point deep behind his eyes.

The searing shock forced a yell from his mouth and bulged his eyes open. The face of a Sioux warrior was inches from his own. Two thick white lines were painted from cheek to cheek and above those his dark eyes were filled with hatred. His left hand gripped Wes's hair, his tugging on which was the cause of the intense pain, and his right held a scalping knife. Unable to defend himself, Wes awaited the searing moment as his scalplock was separated from his head.

A low, guttural voice barked from somewhere behind the brave, causing him to hold back his strike, but the look in his eyes didn't relax. Wes wasn't sure that the command had been uttered with enough authority to permanently prevent the strike. More words were spoken by several voices. Wes was now aware that he was at the centre of a gathering of braves, most of them with lances poised to deter any fight he had in him. There wasn't much. The man astride him hadn't given up hope of taking Wes's life and hair. He began shouting: arguing, Wes supposed, with the man who had reasoned against killing him. With a final cry, his would-be killer raised his knife and stabbed it into the dust adjacent to his left eye.

Wes's gratitude for the man who had argued for his life lasted no more than a moment. Freeing the blade from the ground, his assailant, with a swift, violent jab, smacked the bone handle into the side of his head and, again, Wes lost consciousness.

The next few hours were the most painful and humiliating Wes Gray was ever to endure. He hovered on the edge of consciousness, desperately striving to master his senses. Each time he surfaced from that black chasm it was for only a moment, until the fearful pain in his head forced him to succumb once more to dark oblivion. On the third or fourth occasion he endeavoured to hang on to consciousness, forced himself to learn something of his situation before trying to open his eyes.

He listened for voices, but there were none. The only sound was the steady rumble of unshod horses walking slowly over the dry grassland. He wanted to touch his head, feel the spot which was throbbing with the rhythm of an Indian war drum, but he was unable to move any part of his body. It passed through his mind that he had been paralysed by the injuries he had sustained, that his body could no longer respond to the urgings of his brain.

In panic he opened his eyes. The ground was passing below his head. Wes was mortified by the knowledge that they had tied him, securely, across a pony. His hands were tied together as were his legs, and another rope had been passed under the pony's belly securing wrists to ankles. He tried to raise his head but a wave of pain deterred him from trying too hard. Involuntarily, a groan slipped past his lips. The reward was a blow across his shoulders from a lance or a coup stick. He closed his eyes and when he opened them again it was with a determination to stay conscious and to make some effort to assess the situation.

Blood and dust combined to produce a raging thirst. Blood ran across Wes's brow, over his right eye and lips, and dripped, occasionally, on to the trail below. Somewhere in his misty memory he recalled a gunshot and deduced that to be the cause of the pain in his head. In other circumstances, being merely grazed by a bullet might have been considered lucky but, if the Sioux intended his death to be sport for the village, he could soon be wishing that his death had been instantaneous.

What troubled him was the reason

for their attack. He recalled the face of the warrior who had wanted to scalp him. The hatred in his eyes was almost personal, as though it was Wes and Wes alone whom he wanted to kill. In the jumble of thoughts in his mind he wondered if the two men who had reached Laramie had been telling the truth, wondered if they had been attacked by Sioux, and that somewhere on the plains were two other survivors of the Shoshone raid. Even as that thought occurred to him he knew it was without any real substance. Again he closed his eyes, intending to conserve energy in the hope that an opportunity to escape would present itself.

Whether it was sleep or unconsciousness that overcame him Wes was unable to say, but it was late afternoon when they stopped and the rope that tied him to the pony was cut. Roughly, he was pulled from the animal and thrown to the ground. Because he was bound hand and foot he was unable to protect himself from the impact. His shoulder hit the ground, then his head. He had promised himself not to cry out again, but that was a promise almost broken at the first test.

Suddenly a multitude of legs surrounded him. Men, women and children. The children poked him with sticks, some threw rocks, others kicked or punched. No one spoke, the silent manner of their assault was more frightening than the threat in the hate-filled eyes of the man with the white markings across his nose. He stood over Wes and prodded his shoulder with the blunt end of a lance, eventually striking it hard across his back when Wes tried to turn away from it.

He would have served Wes another blow if the circle hadn't broken to allow two ponies to be led into the ring. An Indian was on the back of each animal, though not riding as to war or the hunt, but slung across the back in the same manner as Wes had been brought to the village. The difference was that their limbs weren't tied, but stuck out, stiff and unmoving. The first body, that of a boy, was lifted down.

Immediately a wail went up from a woman who was pushing her way forward. She took his head, cradling it as those lifting him from the horse put him on the ground. The warrior with the white face markings put down his lance and sank to his knees beside the woman. The sound of her keening was interrupted by another high-pitched shriek as the second body was laid on the ground. Wes could see that this, too, was a young boy, and his mother wailed at the night sky when she saw the terrible gunshot wound that had ended her son's life. To the accompaniment of tom-toms and rattles, women in the crowd began to chant death songs for the boys.

A medicine man hovered over Wes and issued instructions. Two warriors cut the bindings around his wrists and ankles allowing the blood to flow painfully to hands and feet again. They stripped him naked, then marched him around the village, the whiteness of his skin an obvious target for their derision. Wes tried to tell them he was Medicine Feather, brother of the Arapaho and friend of the Sioux, but even with his life at stake, his mouth couldn't form the words nor his lungs summon the strength to make them heard above the tumult.

Sticks and clubs struck blows about his head and body. He began running hoping to avoid most of the blows, but the head wound reopened and blood ran down his forehead and into his right eye. Not that it mattered whether or not he could see, he knew the braves at either side were leading the way to his execution. The air was filled with whoops and high-pitched trills. Men and women wanted revenge for the dead boys. They wanted white man's blood.

Wes was dragged a complete circuit of the village, subjected all the time to threatened blows with knives, lances and tomahawks, and actual blows from clubs and sticks. From time to time he fell but each time he got back up. He wouldn't let them believe they could bully him into submission even though every inch of his body ached and rising to his feet was a signal for the onset of more punishment. Deep inside, however, he knew that to submit to these blows would lessen his worth in the eyes of the warriors and his death, when it came, would be of even greater torment.

When they stopped Wes was back where he had begun, in the centre of the village, near the totem pole. A frame had been erected which was travois-like, one of the sledlike contraptions that their ponies pulled to transport their goods or sick people. As they dragged Wes towards it he found a new reservoir of strength and determination. He stopped, dug in his heels to root himself to the spot, then thrust with all his strength, a last ditch attempt to shake off his captors. The one on the left stumbled but retained a grip on the scout's arm, but there was little effect on the other. He stepped behind Wes and twisted his arm up his back, giving his companion the opportunity to regain his ground.

At the same time the buffalo-horned shaman sprang forward. In his raised hand he carried a bear's claw endowed with long, cruel talons. With a vicious strike he raked the scout's chest, ripping it open with four ragged gashes. Only the guard's tight grip kept Wes upright. Through the haze of pain he heard a scream. For a moment he thought it had come from his own throat, but he was wrong. A warrior charged at him, his lance aimed at the prisoner's heart. Instinctively, Wes knew it was the brave with the white markings and, with that same inner knowledge, he also knew he must be the father of one of the dead boys.

The warrior wasn't allowed to reach Wes. Braves at either side grabbed his arms and dragged him to the ground. A tall Indian, in a feathered bonnet that reached down almost to his knees, stood before him, speaking in a stern voice and silencing the crowd. Everyone listened intently. He ordered the lance to be taken from the man and given to a woman at the front of the circle. She held it while the chief continued talking, his arms and hands gesticulating all the time.

When he stopped the woman threw the lance to the ground, and from the folds of her dress she produced a sharp, short knife. She locked eyes with Wes, then began to sing in a manner that chilled the scout. Another woman moved beside her, she too was holding a knife. They sang together and as they sang the women of the tribe gathered around them. The men, all but the two who held him, moved to one side, clearing the distance between Wes and the women.

The singing stopped abruptly. Slowly, with the elegance of queens on their thrones, the two women seated themselves on the ground. The first woman lifted her head and spoke, throwing her words to the sky. She spoke of her son, of how his spirit now hunted with his ancestors because of the evil that white people had brought to the land of the Lakota. As she reached the end of her speech the knife in her right hand flashed and she chopped the small finger from her left hand. Immediately the second woman followed suit.

Such acts of mutilation were, Wes knew, symbols of mourning. For each dead son the women had removed a finger. They held their hands up to the crowd so they could see the blood flowing over their hands. Everyone began shouting, the men waving war clubs and tomahawks, too. All the anger was aimed at the prisoner.

Wes was pulled to the frame behind him, his legs spread wide and fastened at the ankles. Likewise his arms were stretched out above his head and tied at the wrists. In vain he struggled. Had he been uninjured his resistance might have been greater, but the outcome was inevitable. There were too many to fight. It took only seconds for them to secure him to the poles, to string him up in the dying heat of the day like the carcass of a deer waiting to be butchered.

The villagers dispersed, leaving him to the agonies of his body. Blood now flowed not only from the head wound but also from the savage slashes inflicted by the medicine man. In addition, his back, shoulders and head had taken a series of heavy blows as he'd run the village gauntlet. Bloody sweat dripped into his eyes and every breath seemed like a swallow of barbed wire in his parched throat.

He was left to hang in torment. At some point he passed out, only to be revived by the medicine man, who shouted in his face and threatened again to use the sharp talons of the bear claw that he carried. Wes had slumped so that his arms were bearing all his weight. The pain in the shoulder joints was barely eased by the little adjustments it was possible to make.

By now the sun was low and would soon disappear. The medicine man began cajoling some braves. In a short time they began to stack kindling in preparation for a big fire. With an eerie fascination Wes watched as the village people began to congregate around the totem pole. Some were wrapped in blankets, others carried them over their arm. It seemed that the party would not soon be over. The time had come, Wes realized, for his death, and it was a cause for celebration.

When the last rays of that day's sun touched the ground the drums began. The people sat in a circle around the unlit fire and listened while the old men sang. Then the chief stood up, casting aside the blanket he carried so that he could exhort the people of the village with gestures as well as with words. His wiry frame was short and his voice was a flat monotone, but he wore a long, feathered bonnet which touched the ground and gave authority to his presence and words.

For the most part Wes couldn't understand the Indian's speech, but from time to time the chief pointed at the prisoner. There was nothing in his manner to suggest he was exhorting the tribe to murder and, for a moment, Wes thought that perhaps he was being defended, that the chief was telling his people that the captive had not been allowed to speak in his own defence or explain his reason for being in the land of the Sioux, but it was a hope that was short-lived.

The medicine man stepped forward again, with something clasped in his hands. Wes could see water running to the ground as the Indian approached. Whatever he was holding, it clearly wouldn't bring any comfort to the captive. At that moment, Wes lost all expectation of mercy. By now the particular torments of wounds and thirst had left him, only the desire for life survived.

The medicine man passed behind Wes and he felt the Indian's damp hands wrapping something around his throat. It tied the scout to the frame, tightly, so that he couldn't move his head. Everyone fell silent. Wes recognized the feel of rawhide on his skin. Wet rawhide shrinks as it dries. Somewhere behind him an order was shouted. Within seconds the great fire was lit. The fire's heat would cause his slow strangulation. As the medicine man moved away from him he could see that many of the women had knives. Before he was dead the women would be allowed to take revenge for the death of the children.

It didn't take long for the fire's heat to take effect. The excess water that had splashed on his shoulders and chest from the soaked rawhide dried in seconds. Within minutes Wes could feel the rawhide biting into his neck. He breathed deeply through his nose.

Swallowing was painful. The medicine man danced, waving his rattle, chanting his words, passing before the victim's eyes a lance adorned with many dry scalps. Wes tried not to look at them but it was impossible to move his head. He grunted for air as the choker tightened.

An arrow thudded into the frame above his head, then, accompanied by a single wild yell, another struck, eye-high, in the angle between his upraised right arm and his head. Breathing hurt. It felt as though the shrinking rawhide was cutting through Wes's neck. His vision was blurred. Sounds were blending into a rushing wind which climaxed with the excited cries of the women. His lungs were close to bursting, his windpipe was almost crushed. He was gagging for air.

At that point, when he was unsure whether his lungs or his heart would be the first to burst, the binding around his neck was cut and his head lolled forward. With painful gasps he sucked in air. The sound in his throat matched that of the rattle carried by the medicine man. Wes wanted to rub his throat, massage it to open the passageway to his lungs. He needed to bend his body so that he could take in more air. But movement of all kind was impossible. His lungs ached, his heart pounded and it felt as though a wild stallion had trampled on his windpipe.

Then water splashed in his face, concentrating his thoughts on the senses of life. The roaring in his ears subsided and he realized that the only sounds he could hear were the crackling of the fire and his own laboured breathing. He opened his eyes. Gradually he was able to focus on the figure before him. It was the chief, uncaring of the prisoner's pain, unexcited by his torment, stoically examining his face. When he was certain that Wes recognized him he indicated with his lance for the medicine man to come forward. Wes prayed that the ordeal was over.

Water dripped again from the advancing Medicine Man's hands. Silently he tied a new strip of rawhide around the scout's throat. This done, he raised his arms and emitted a wild yell. Despite the pain, Wes breathed deeply, clinging dearly to life, but already his lungs felt as though they were trying to break through his ribcage. His eyes closed, but only for a moment. A sharp blow struck his forehead, followed by another on his neck. A throng of braves had formed around him, each one determined to strike him, to add to his humiliation in retribution for the killing of the boys. The tom-toms were thudding and the night was filled with whoops and trills of a celebrating village.

It seemed that the rawhide did its work more quickly the second time, or perhaps Wes was just less resilient. He passed out with the accumulation of blows and slow asphyxiation.

For a second time he was revived and, when the chief had assured himself again that Wes was aware of what was happening, he signalled once more to the medicine man. Though the binding around his throat had been released and he was able to breathe air into his body, the pressure and pain Wes felt was no less severe. As the shaman tied the wet rawhide a third time, Wes knew it would be the last.

This time, the medicine man's wild yell brought the women to their feet. Through the flames their knives glinted. Though the tom-toms continued their beat the people were silent. Two women advanced and stood before Wes, watching the rawhide tighten and dig into the taut skin at his throat. The last breath was being choked out of him. In his pain and loss of consciousness, noises blurred together and faces became indistinguishable. But the women were moving as a throng. With his last thought he knew they were coming for him.

8

In the blackness brought about by slow asphyxiation, Wes Gray's body wouldn't have registered the pain from the expected slashes of mutilation, nor his mind acknowledge that one telling blow of death. As the women advanced, the leaping flames of the council fire glinting off their short, sharp knives, Wes succumbed without resistance to the darkness of oblivion. His last vexations before being swallowed by the great void were that the wagons would have to face the crossing of the Platte without him and that there was no way back to Little Feather, the Arapaho girl who shared his tepee in the village on the Snake.

He had undertaken a great journey, a strange journey in a world in which there was nothing. There were no landmarks to signpost the way or mark his passing. There were no people to speak to or animals to follow, no trees or plants to provide shade or sustenance. He had no horse beneath him, or wagon to ride, or canoe to carry him, but he needed none of those for there was neither land nor water beneath him. Yet it was indeed a journey, though he needed no food or drink or weapons or tools to tackle it. All he needed was the belief to proceed without trepidation and trust that his destination was not to be feared.

Sudden sounds scattered the nothingness like a gunshot scatters geese. Colours flashed before his eyes. Red, black and yellow. But still there was no guiding light to shine the way ahead. There was no surface to swim to, no summit to scale. From time to time there seemed to be flashes of the real world. Shapes, like wraiths, lingered, swaying close, and on each occasion bringing with them the pattern of red and black and yellow. In those brief moments he knew again the pain he had suffered at the hands of the Sioux; a dull reminder, he supposed, that he was to carry with him into the hereafter.

When his eyes opened they did so like those of a cougar disturbed by an unfamiliar sound. He lay still, knowing it was important to gather whatever information he could about his present situation. Befuddled, and because his last conscious thought had been of death, the words of a preacher reading over a cousin's coffin filled his head: *In my Father's house there are many rooms . . .*

It took a few seconds to shake off the notion that this might be one of those rooms. He had expected rather more of Heaven than the rustic furniture by which he was now surrounded.

He moved his head so that he could see through a partly open door that led into another room. Wes closed his eyes, a necessary act because the images were becoming blurred and beginning to spin. He breathed deeply, controlling the pace of his heartbeats, giving his other senses the opportunity to gather information.

The overriding sensation was one of pain, especially a tightness about his throat. Remembrance of the thrice-applied rawhide strip flooded his mind. He raised his fingers to his neck and traced the deep groove that had been formed. He swallowed, expecting and experiencing pain. Though it hardly seemed possible, it confirmed that he was alive. For a moment he imagined himself still bound to the frame of poles, once again he saw the firelight glinting on the blades of the advancing women.

The thought of their intentions gripped his stomach like an icy hand and, grateful though he was to have survived, the possibilities of what the women had done to him brought a sweat to his brow. He moved gingerly, but that excited pain in almost every part of his body. His back and shoulders had borne the burden of the

151

beating when running their gauntlet and now the resulting swellings and abrasions were becoming a growing source of torment.

One by one he checked off his faculties. The realization that his sight and hearing were intact eased away his worries. With difficulty he moved his tongue. The combination of thirst and the effects of strangulation made it difficult to speak, but he managed to produce a hoarse sound, which was evidence that maybe no permanent damage had been done.

Cautiously he raised the blanket. Long leaves from river rushes covered his chest: from beneath them a green unguent oozed: an Indian remedy that had been smeared on his body to cure the cuts inflicted by the medicine man. Raising the blanket higher, he was able to see all the way to his toes. He was still naked, but there were no other wounds.

Then he realized that someone's voice was carrying to him from outdoors. The severity of its monotone, coupled with the aroma of coffee coming from the adjoining room, provided Wes with a clue to where he now was. The voice he could hear belonged to Jim Taylor; although no other voice was raised in argument against him, Jim's tone was strident, angry, threatening.

Wes tried to sit up but a pain as agonizing as any that he had experienced shot through his head. With a groan he lowered it to the pillow. When he put his hand to his brow he discovered that a poultice, putty-like and ill-smelling, similar to those on his chest, had been applied to the head wound. While he was inspecting the greenish unguent, the door to the room opened wider and Jim's wife, Apo Hopa, entered.

Her expression showed concern, but Wes suspected that it was not all for him. Her glance towards the window betrayed the fact that she was also worried about the events that were happening outside. She'd brought with her a bowl of water from which she allowed Wes two sips. Then she placed her cool hand on his brow and, miraculously, for him the room stopped spinning.

Having thus attained a more settled state of mind Wes was anxious to have his questions answered. With swift hand movements and few words the Sioux girl told him what she knew. He had been saved from death by her brother, who had returned to the village with the stolen ponies and many scalps. Throws The Dust had identified Wes as *Wiyaka Wakan*, Medicine Feather of the Arapaho, and declared that it was he who had directed the Ogallalah warriors to the camp of the Shoshone raiders. Although his life had been spared, Wes wondered if the Sioux still harboured plans to punish other white people for the slaying of the boys.

'Red Knife will not permit it,' Apo Hopa told him, 'but Black Raven and Pawnee Killer, the fathers of the dead boys, still want revenge. They will challenge Red Knife's leadership. If they win they will follow the warpath.'

It occurred to Wes that the sound of Jim Taylor's harangue had been going on ever since he'd regained consciousness. Now Jim's tone was rising, he was spitting forth a mighty torrent of abuse and threat, like the cant of a hell-fire preacher. Sky turned her head towards the sound, worry-lines crinkled her brow and concern gleamed in her eyes.

'Who is he shouting at?' Wes asked.

'My people,' she said. 'A hunting party. Throws The Dust rides with them. He came to see if you have recovered.'

'Why doesn't he come in?'

'My husband will not let him into the house. He doesn't welcome anyone. He stands with gun. My people think he will shoot them.'

'Surely not your brother?'

'My brother. My father. Even white soldiers when they come.'

'Is he not made welcome when he

visits Red Knife's village?'

'We never go. We haven't been since he took me from Grey Moccasin's tepee.'

Wes couldn't believe that Jim Taylor had spurned the opportunity for friendship with Sky's people. Whatever thoughts were occupying his mind, they were isolating him more than the land or weather ever could. Wes felt sorry for Sky. She had given up her family and friends to live with a man unprepared to adapt to his surroundings. On his previous visit Wes hadn't heard him utter one word of Sioux or use even the most common signs of the Plains tribes.

Almost as though she could read his thoughts Apo Hopa signed that her husband was a good man.

Well, Wes thought, *it certainly sounds as though he is prepared to protect her and fight for her.* But he wasn't convinced that that was all Sky wanted.

'Now I must go,' she said. 'Throws The Dust waits for me to tell him that all is well.'

Wes touched the poultice on his brow. 'And is it?'

She smiled, pressed her fingers against the hand she was holding.

'It is well,' she said. 'I must go.'

It wasn't easy but, when Apo Hopa left the bedroom Wes sat up, determined to ignore the wooziness in his head and to find out for himself what was happening outside. In these circumstances he didn't think that shouting at the Sioux was the wisest thing to do, not even for Jim Taylor, whose reason had been sorely affected by the loneliness of the plains.

Although the Sioux had great tolerance for those who were eccentric, or just plain crazy, Wes also knew that that tolerance, based on the religious belief that such people had been singled out by *Waka Tanka*, the Great Spirit, would be instantly terminated if the madness turned to violence.

Furthermore, Jim Taylor wasn't a Sioux, and, apart from taking Sky as his wife, had never shown any respect for her people. Some from the village were looking for the scalps of white men to avenge the deaths of Little Otter and Pony Holder. Even those who did not share the warlike views of Black Raven and Pawnee Killer would be angry over the killing of the boys.

It hadn't escaped Wes Gray's attention that the deaths of the two boys could also be bad news for the wagon train. Who had killed the boys, and why, were immaterial to Black Raven and his supporters. Two of their children were dead and they didn't care whose life was taken in return. The next prisoner might not have anyone to intercede on his behalf, as Throws The Dust had done for him. The fact that the wagons were several days' journey from the spot where the killings took place would be of no significance if the Sioux rode in that direction. Wes considered it imperative to get a warning to Caleb Dodge.

Using the wall and whatever furniture he could reach for support, he made his way, naked, out of the bedroom. Progress wasn't easy and he stumbled more than once, cursing as the door between the rooms seemed to shift position after every step. When eventually he stumbled into the main room he was surprised to find another person in there.

She turned and gasped at the scout's sudden appearance. Her eyes widened and her hands flew to her mouth, as if to suggest that the tumult in the yard was less threatening to her than the naked man across the room.

Wes studied the girl for a moment, taking in the long red travelling dress, which was in need of some attention. The fabric was torn in several places, and dust and grime clung to it. Her face, too, showed signs of an ordeal. Patches of discoloration — the results of physical abuse by Clem Butler — emphasized the paleness of her skin.

Even so, Wes recalled the photograph Captain O'Malley had found in the abandoned stagecoach and the conversation he'd had with Sky's brother. He muttered words intended merely to prompt his own fractured memory but spoken loud enough for the girl to hear.

'Ellie Rogers?'

The girl's eyes widened further, her hands remained in front of her mouth. She nodded. She was younger than Wes had expected and, despite the bruises and cuts, prettier.

They studied each other for an instant but Wes's attention was soon drawn back to the argument going on beyond the threshold, where Jim Taylor was declaring that the land and everything on it were his, and that no thievin' Injun was taking it from him.

Wes crossed the room to the open doorway. Jim was standing to his right, almost at the corner of the cabin. He held his rifle across his body, prepared to turn it on anyone who stepped out of line. Facing him, in that familiar semi-circle formation, were ten mounted Sioux warriors. Wes recognized some of them. They were watching Jim Taylor in chilling silence, their expressions as impassive as their ponies were motionless.

As long as Jim did no more than shout and gesticulate there was little danger to him. The Sioux understood not a word he was saying, nor the meaning of his wildly waving hands. Bemused by his voice and movement, they believed him to be touched by a spirit. One day, they expected, the power that he had been given would be revealed.

That was why they watched in silence now and why they had watched him from the hills in the past. If the power was for good and peace they would honour him. If it ever changed to bring evil and violence they would kill him.

Sky was standing beside her husband now, holding his arm to make it difficult for him to raise his rifle. She was talking to him, pleading with him to return to the house; but, just as the

Sioux didn't understand his words, so her exhortations were meaningless to him. Even if he could have taken them in it was probably too late; Jim Taylor was beyond listening to reason. The delusions in his mind had control of him and concealed from him any threat to his life.

The appearance of Wes Gray in the doorway distracted the Sioux from the raving farmer. The warrior at the end of the line turned to face Wes. It was Throws The Dust; his face was completely painted with broad bands of red, black and yellow, as it had been when they'd spoken at the creek, and as had been the combination of colours that had occasionally presented itself to Wes during his unconscious journey from the Indian village.

'*A-Hey!*' shouted Throws The Dust, half as a greeting and half as an exclamation of surprise. He had come expecting to see Wes covered with blankets, yet here he was, on his feet and stretching out an arm in a gesture

of welcome. Performing the arm movement was awkward and painful because
of the injuries to his shoulders and
chest, but Wes did it in full. If he was to
continue travelling the trails through
Sioux territory it was essential that the
warriors retained respect for him. He
could not appear weak and defeated.

Using the porch rail for support, he
kept his head high and his back
straight. He had to show that his spirit
had not been broken by the ordeal
suffered in their village. They had to
understand his strength and determination: that he would either be a brave
ally, or a dangerous enemy. Though
waves of dizziness threatened to topple
him to the ground, he stood firm,
knowing that, from his pony, Throws
The Dust was examining the bruises
and bindings on his head and upper
body.

The slight breeze disturbed the
feathers and decorations on the lances
and war shields of the gathered
Lakotas. They fluttered and jingled,

giving rise to the lightest music, a faint mix of whistle and drum. Throws The Dust spoke.

'Wiyaka Wakan is very strong. Only the bravest warrior would be standing after such wounds. In the village we will speak of our friend Medicine Feather. His name will be honoured tonight around our campfires.'

'And what of the Shoshones, Throws The Dust? Did you find them?'

'The death of Kicking Bear has been avenged and our ponies graze once more beside Lakota tepees.' He raised his lance above his head which evoked a chorus of excited yelps from the mounted warriors behind. Wes could see fresh scalps attached to many of their lances and shields and figured that not many of the Shoshone raiding party had returned to their own village.

Not every brave in the group was happy to salute Wes. Suddenly, in the very moment that the visit of the Sioux seemed happily resolved, the air became brittle with tension. Nothing could disguise the hatred reflected in the black eyes of the brave who now walked his horse forward, and nothing screamed danger like the two white lines which crossed his nose from cheek to cheek. Black Raven halted beside Throws The Dust.

'Go,' he told Wes. 'Leave our land. No white man will be honoured in the lodges where mothers cry for dead sons. Around the council fire tonight we will decide for war. In the morning all white men will be our enemy.'

Throws The Dust spoke to Black Raven. 'You do not decide for our people. Red Knife speaks against war.'

'Red Knife speaks like an old woman. The Lakota are warriors. They need a chief who has no fear of his enemies.'

After speaking these words Black Raven hefted his lance and flung it towards Wes. It passed over his head and thudded into the timber wall to the left of the doorway. The lance wasn't meant to kill; throwing it had been a ritual, needed for Black Raven to show his intentions to the other warriors, needed to prove his bravery, although what bravery was needed to attack Wes at that moment was questionable. Still, it was a threat.

Only Red Knife's word was holding Black Raven in check, and Wes knew that it was only the presence of Throws The Dust that guaranteed that no one would try to kill him this day. Jim Taylor knew no such thing. Sky had relaxed her grip on his arm while her brother talked, and now, as Black Raven hurled his weapon, Jim swung his rifle to his shoulder and aimed at the Indian. Sky screamed and pushed his arm, sending the shot into the air. Up to that point Wes had suspected that Black Raven had little support for his calls for war against the white man, but now he realized the tension felt by all the Sioux. At the report from Jim Taylor's rifle the Sioux ponies shuffled and stamped and suddenly arrows were flying. Jim's rifle fell to the ground and he staggered back against the porch rail. For several seconds he leaned against it with four arrows in his chest. Then, crumpling, he slid to the ground and died looking at the sky.

Throws The Dust waved his arms and shouted at his comrades, some of whom regarded Wes with dreadful meaning. Naked and unarmed he had no means of defending himself. His guns, he assumed, were in the house. He would never reach them. But Throws The Dust was in command. The Sioux braves listened while he berated them.

'Are you women to kill such a one? His mind has left him. Do the warriors of the Lakota no longer protect those who are weakened?'

'Only our own,' grunted one of the braves.

'He was our own,' said Throws The Dust. 'Chosen by my sister to be her husband and honoured by Grey Moccasin, our father, who gave her as his wife.'

When the ponies were still again and

the murmurs had ceased Throws The Dust dismounted and stood beside his sister. Sky was kneeling beside her dead husband singing a death chant. Throws The Dust rested a hand on her shoulder.

'You must come with us now.'

She shook her head. 'I must mourn my husband.'

'There will be trouble,' he told her. 'Soldiers will come.'

'This is my home. I must mourn properly. Then I will return to the village.'

'You cannot stay long,' her brother said. 'Soon I will come for you.'

She bowed her head and began again to chant the death song.

Throws The Dust turned his attention to Wes, approaching him with quick, aggressive steps, his expression difficult to read.

'There will be fighting because of this. You must go quickly.'

'No,' said Wes. 'There need be no more fighting. I will tell the soldiers what happened here. They won't punish your people.'

'A white man has been killed. When the soldiers hear of this the Lakota will be punished.'

'I am Medicine Feather, brother of the Arapaho and friend of the Sioux. I will speak to the soldiers for my friends. Let there be no more fighting.'

'I am not the chief of my village,' replied the Indian. 'I cannot say what will happen. But the talk around the council fire will be of more things than revenge for the death of Little Otter and Pony Holder. There is much talk of soldiers moving into the *Paha Sapa*. If fighting is the only way we can keep the land that is ours then there will be war.'

Black Raven pushed his pony alongside Throws The Dust. He sat astride it, his back straight, his head high and a gleam of satisfaction in his eyes.

'It begins,' he told Wes. 'When we meet again I will kill you.' With those words he turned his horse and led the other riders away from the cabin, their wild yelps carried on the breeze as they galloped towards the hills and home.

After the dust of the Indian ponies had settled on the skyline, Wes and Throws The Dust turned their attention to Apo Hopa. She knelt on the ground, arms outstretched in supplication to the Great Spirit to take her husband on the path to *Wangi Yata*, the Land of Great Shadows. Unlike the mothers of Pony Holder and Little Otter, Apo Hopa's sadness was not marked with high-pitched wails. When her chants were completed she straightened his limbs and turned him so that his body pointed to the sun. Then she fetched some water from the rain barrel and washed the dust from his face, as though preparing him for an important journey.

Wes watched Sky, knowing that for the moment she would work alone. In an Indian village the work of tending to the dead was woman's work and Sky would neither need nor want any help from Throws The Dust or himself. He was impressed by the calm manner in which she attended to her husband's body, and he hoped that her restrained mourning signified that she would not commit some later act of self-mutilation such as had been performed by the mothers of the dead boys.

'Throws The Dust,' Wes said, 'you must continue to speak against war. I'm the only white man who knows how Jim died and I'm not going to tell anyone. I'll bury him before I leave here. No one is going to dig him up again. Tell Red Knife that no soldiers will come to punish the Sioux.'

'I will tell Red Knife, but this doesn't mean there will not be war. Black Raven and Pawnee Killer have many friends who are angry that their vengeance has been denied. If Black Raven becomes chief he will lead his braves on revenge raids against the white people.'

'You must prevent that. Tell the council that I know who killed the boys. They have killed white people, too. You know them, Throws The Dust. They are the men who took the woman. The one with hair on his face the colour of my horse and his partner. They are in Laramie. When I return there they will be caught and punished. You have the word of Medicine Feather.'

For a moment the Sioux warrior considered what Wes had said, then he touched his chest in the sign of friendship and rode away. Wes returned to the cabin, found his clothes and got dressed. He reflected on the fact that there was no better medicine for his own ailments than someone else's death. That was not to say that seeing Jim Taylor with a chest full of arrows cured his own pains, but for the most part it made him forget them. When he did feel them they reminded him that he'd survived and would recover.

Wes buried Jim Taylor on a small rise about thirty yards from the cabin. Sky sang her song while he worked. She had changed her clothing. The dull, rough buckskin dress she had worn earlier was replaced by a soft, fringed leather dress which was almost white in colour. It was decorated with beads and the fur of small animals, which had been dyed a tender blue.

The moccasins on her feet were, like her dress, softer and paler than those she had worn earlier, and her hair was freshly braided and held in place with a rabbit-hide band.

She carried a small, brightly coloured doll made of buffalo hide and as she sang she raised it above her head as if in offering to her gods. Clearly the doll was important in her mourning, though whether it was significant to Jim Taylor alone or was part of the usual Ogallalah ceremony wasn't clear to Wes. What was clear to him, however, was the girl's beauty. Repeatedly, as he worked, his eyes strayed to where she knelt, finding pleasure in the high cheekbones and big, dark eyes.

Such thoughts troubled Wes but Apo Hopa's future was uppermost in his mind. When he looked up Sky's gaze was upon him, her eyes steady as they studied the lines of his face, as though she were reading his thoughts and was pleased with them. He smiled at her.

'There is much to do,' he said, and stood over the grave. There wasn't time to make a marker and there didn't seem any reason to speak words so, when they were done, they went back to the cabin.

'Fee?' asked Sky. Wes shook his head, which made him wince. Sky made him sit so that she could examine the head wound. She wasn't distressed by what she saw but renewed the poultice with a concoction of herbs and berries, which she mashed in a clay mortar and worked into a paste-like substance with the addition of some form of animal grease and her own saliva.

Ellie Rogers, who hadn't left the cabin at any time, sat silently, watching Sky at work. Wes regarded her long, stained travelling dress.

'We need to find you something else to wear,' he told her. 'You'll never get astride a horse dressed like that.'

Ellie looked at him as though seeing him as an ally for the first time.

'Who are you?'

'My name is Wes Gray. I've been looking for you since the hold-up. You were lucky that Throws The Dust found you. He's Sky's brother.'

Next morning, at Wes Gray's prompting, Sky found some of Jim Taylor's clothes for Ellie to wear. There was a blue plaid shirt and some grey woollen trousers which were less than flattering for the slim young girl. Both shirt and trousers were too large and Ellie could only accommodate herself to them by rolling up the sleeves and trouser legs. Wes had to cut a length of rope to tie around Ellie's waist to keep the trousers in place and he supplied her with the floppy, grey hat he'd found, into which she bundled her thick, red hair.

Ellie's appearance was inelegant but more than practical for the journey to the fort. While Sky and Ellie busied themselves with the wardrobe, Wes went to the barn to saddle the animals. The Sioux had returned both Red and the stray that had found him by the creek. Now they were well fed and rested, and keen to be saddled up and exercised. Wes led the horses to the front of the cabin and called for the women.

'I must get Ellie back to the fort,' he told Sky when she emerged. 'What will you do?'

'I will mourn my husband,' she said. 'Tomorrow I will return to Red Knife's village.' She touched the scout's arm. 'Will you return?' Her dark eyes asked questions that were deeper than her words, questions that were impossible to answer. Who could say when he would again be welcome in a Sioux village?

But he kissed her before leaving.

9

Having witnessed the shooting of Wes
Gray and watched long enough to see
his spread-eagled body surrounded by
Indians, Lew Butler and Charlie Huntz
thought all their problems had been
solved. The only man with the ability to
track them from the scene of the
hold-up to the Laramie stage depot
was, they believed, dead. Their secret
was safe and they had a sackful of
money to share. Without definite plans,
they had returned to the scattering of
buildings near Fort Laramie in high
spirits, determined to put on a show of
bravado for the citizens there.

Jed and Clara Clancy had heard the
wagon scout threaten Lew and, in view
of Wes Gray's reputation, they expected
the newcomers to move on without
delay. It was with some surprise,
therefore, that they found the two

cattlemen still hanging around their liquor room a couple of days later, drinking, gambling and declaring that no Injun lover would chase them from any place they wanted to stay. Jed told his wife that such talk was plumb foolish.

'I ain't sure if they're foolish or just spoiling for a fight,' said Clara. 'There's something mean about those two.'

'Tough trail hands they may be,' said her husband, 'but their lives won't be worth a plugged nickel if they're still here when Wes Gray returns. People are paying heed to their talk and anticipating a fight. Somebody is sure to tell Wes. His temper's got a mighty short fuse when it comes to badmouthing Indians. Don't matter which tribe, neither.'

Jed was right about people taking notice of Lew and Charlie's behaviour. They'd gained a certain status in the settlement because of their oft-repeated account of their stand against the Sioux. Few of Laramie's inhabitants hadn't heard the tale at first hand; many of them were eager to praise the pair for their fighting ability.

The threat of war with the tribes of the Plains still hung over the smattering of settlers whose homesteads were scattered north towards the Black Hills. It seemed that from day to day their opinions of the correct solution to the Indian problem swung between two extremes. Either teach them to live like Americans or kill them all. Some incidents, like the one described with bias by Lew Butler and Charlie Huntz, aroused fighting talk, but much of the early interest in their exploits was withdrawn when the Laramie people learned of Wes Gray's threat.

Although there were some in the community who had no liking for Wes Gray's association with the tribes, there were none who would voice that opinion within earshot of him. They might not like his lifestyle but it didn't affect their respect for his abilities. His reputation as a fighting man was not in doubt. So, it was the general opinion that the two cowboys would be wise to continue their journey to the cattle country of Wyoming, and many an eyebrow was raised when they remained and voiced challenges to Wes Gray for everyone to hear. Their careless behaviour attracted the attention of one person in particular: Curly Clayport, the Wells Fargo agent.

When Captain O'Malley brought news of the stagecoach hold-up to his attention, Curly's thoughts had at first been focused on relaying details of the robbery to Cheyenne and considering plans to track down the robbers in hopes of reclaiming the stolen money. There was also a kidnapped passenger to rescue. The safe return of both of these was essential for the reputation of the company but, Curly knew, the chances of recovering either diminished with each passing hour. It was impossible to organize a posse from the citizens of this hamlet, there being insufficient men of suitable calibre, and the army wouldn't interfere in what was strictly a civilian affair. By the time men could arrive from Cheyenne it was probable that all trace of a trail would be lost.

The only gleam of light for Curly was Wes Gray. The wagon scout's being guided to Fort Laramie at that particular moment had been, he reasoned, the act of a kindly God. Life in a frontier settlement wasn't easy: Curly fought and cursed and killed when necessary but whatever religion he could afford he adhered to. So long as it didn't interfere with his job, his few pleasures or his neighbour's opinion that he was a fine man of the West, he would admit to a Christian faith that had served him well all his years. Wes Gray's arrival was further proof that Curly could witness to the existence of a Power that watched over God-fearing people.

Like everyone who had lived in Laramie for several years, he was aware of Wes Gray's reputation. The report that he had gone in pursuit of the robbers offered hope for some kind of success. If anyone could bring back either money or captive it was Wes Gray.

Which was why he was needled by the derogatory remarks made by Lew Butler and Charlie Huntz. Wes Gray had less reason than most people hereabouts to go after the killers of the agent's stagecoach driver and guard; the crime affected the people of Laramie more than him; it had been committed in their territory, not his. Jake Welchman and Ben Garland had been driving the coach through Laramie for more years than Curly could remember; he figured their violent deaths should be arousing folks hereabout to greater action than a sorrowful remembrance as they raised their glasses of beer.

Furthermore, that kidnapped girl was due to be the soldier's bride. No doubt the military had to obey orders and leave the hunt for her abductors to civil law but there was nothing to prevent that young captain from taking a few days' leave and burning up the land between here and the Platte in an effort to find her. The stolen money? Well that, no doubt, was the payroll for the silver-mine workers in Cheyenne. Perhaps they'd send someone to investigate the holdup but too much time had passed for them to have much hope of success.

There was, however, nothing to stop those newcomers, Butler and Huntz, from mounting up and helping in the search, yet they hadn't shown any enthusiasm for anything other than cards and whiskey since arriving in Laramie. Curly would have held them in higher esteem if, instead of bad-mouthing Wes Gray, they had saddled their horses and ridden with him to help in the search.

With a shrug, Curly threw back the last of the whiskey in his glass. He considered the two men again and wondered if his judgement of them was too harsh. They had, after all, fought off a Sioux war party. That was no mean feat and deserving of a few days' celebration. He threw another look in their direction, noted the pile of dollar notes in front of them on the table: winnings from their recent poker game with two of the settlement's citizens, and told himself they were the richest drovers he'd ever seen.

One of them, the elder one, the one called Lew, removed his hat, spun it in his hands and inspected the hatband with its neat collection of silver discs. Curly had to admit it was a smart hat. He admired it. He remembered admiring a similar one a few weeks earlier and it had been nagging at him for two days as he tried to recall who else had had such a hat. Now, as Jake Clancy poured more whiskey into his glass the image of Jake Welchman, with his hat clutched to his chest, leapt into his mind.

The recollection startled Curly. Of course he couldn't be certain it was the same hat but it had also been a new one. He'd only worn it that one time — on his last trip through from Cheyenne. Proud as a peacock he'd been, adjusting it from one angle to another, or whipping it off and clutching it to his chest whenever he spoke to a female or anyone of authority. Still, Curly argued with himself, just because it had a fancy hatband didn't mean it was unique. If Jake had ordered his from a catalogue there could be dozens like it all over the Western states, but Curly mused on the coincidence. As Lew Butler counted the discs on the hatband, Curly had an uncomfortable feeling that the hat *had* belonged to his stagecoach guard.

As though taking his cue from Curly's thoughts, Charlie Huntz spoke to his partner.

'You sure like that hat, Lew.'

Lew grinned. 'Couldn't have found a better one.'

Overhearing their conversation and hoping to elicit some useful snippet that would help him decide the hat's provenance, Curly joined in.

'I was admiring it myself. May I ask where you got it?'

Lew put the hat back on his head.

'Picked it up someplace.' Lew grinned, but there wasn't a lot of mirth in it. He was thoughtful, watchful when Curly pressed on with his interest.

'Where exactly was that? I might like to get one of those myself.'

'Can't remember the name of the place,' said Lew. 'Just somewhere along the trail.'

'Not Abilene?'

'No. Certainly not Abilene.' There was no longer any humour in Lew's voice.

Aware that his questions had irked the man, Curly departed, his final words intended as an affable end to the conversation.

'Guess I'll just have to settle for a plain one like those that Jed stocks in the back room.'

After he'd gone, Lew spoke softly and urgently to Charlie Huntz.

'I think that Wells Fargo guy is on to us. He was mighty interested in this hat.'

'Do you think he recognized it?'

'Could be.' Lew's voice carried a dark, sinister edge.

'What are we going to do about it?' Charlie's question held the implication that killing Curly Clayport was the only sensible solution.

'Time to move on, I reckon,' replied Lew. 'We'll go at first light, collect the money we stashed away and head on down to Denver. We'll have some fun there, then you go head for the riverboats while I make tracks to 'Frisco.'

'What about that Wells Fargo man? We just gonna forget about him?'

'Seems like the best idea. He may have suspicions about our involvement with the robbery but no proof. And that scout ain't bringing any to him.'

Lew stopped examining his hat and

put it back on his head. 'Wells Fargo will soon put two and two together if our leaving Laramie coincided with the killing of their agent. Our descriptions would be in every lawman's office in the territory. No, Charlie, we won't do anything to Mr Curly Clayport. Instead, we'll leave before sunup. If anyone comes looking for us, they'll go chasing out along the trail to Wyoming, where we told everyone we were headed, and in the meantime we'll be cutting out the miles to Denver.'

With that decision made they were packed and gone from their hotel rooms after only a couple of hours' sleep. Their advance room hire had been sufficient to cover another two nights, so there was no need to inform the hotel clerk of their departures. Accordingly, they were saddled up before the first hint of daylight illuminated the high wood-frame stable. Intending to keep their departure a secret for as long as possible, they led their horses to the edge of town before mounting and riding south.

They didn't go unobserved. One other person in the stage-stop settlement was awake. Troubled by suspicion and indecision, Curly Clayport paced the small front room of the building that served as his home and the Wells Fargo office. He was certain that the cavalry had brought back Jake Welchman's body bareheaded. After breakfast, he decided, his first task would be to get confirmation of that fact from Captain O'Malley. If it turned out that the guard's hat had indeed been missing when they found him he would consult with Colonel Flint on a course of action. Of course the colonel would take the official line. *Civilian matter*, he would say, *nothing I can do about it.*

But unofficially he could summon Lew Butler and Charlie Huntz to the fort on the pretext of gathering information on the movement of hostile tribesmen. With luck, he would detain them long enough for Curly to telegraph Cheyenne. Two days of swift riding would bring a territorial marshal to the settlement. The matter would then be his responsibility.

Satisfied in his mind that his plan was both prudent and practical, Curly turned out his lamp in the hope of grabbing an hour of sleep before the settlement came to life. At that moment he heard the slow, steady step of walking horses. Surprised that anyone was abroad so early, he opened the shutter at the window. The blackness of the night was easing into a muggy, pre-dawn grey. Curly screwed up his eyes in concentration. Sure enough, somebody was out on the street, moving slowly and stealthily.

Silently he opened the office door and stepped out on to the boardwalk. Although there was insufficient light to discern the details of the faces of the two men, their shape and movement betrayed their identity. From among the handful of people in this small, stage-stop settlement it wasn't difficult to recognize Lew Butler and Charlie Huntz. They were quitting the settlement and doing so in secrecy. At the end of the street they stopped, mounted, then galloped away towards the foothills that led to the long-grass country.

Curly Clayport wouldn't have called himself a brave man. When younger he'd been in several skirmishes, fist fights and gunfights, but it wasn't something he bragged about or relished having to repeat. But at that moment he knew he had no alternative but to follow Lew Butler and Charlie Huntz. It was his duty to catch them, confront them with his suspicions about the robbery and retrieve the stolen money. Yes, it was his duty to do that, and, moreover, Ben Garland and Jake Welchman had been his friends and he was determined that their killers wouldn't go unpunished. He was sure they hadn't done anything to deserve the violence that had been meted out to them. He strapped on his gunbelt and checked that his pistol was fully loaded. Then he grabbed a rifle from a wall rack and raced out to the stable. He saddled his bay mare quickly and set off in pursuit.

He didn't go too fast. Without sight of them it would be rash to proceed too quickly. Until there was a little light he would refrain from headlong pursuit. If they heard someone on their back trail they could easily set an ambush. No, for the moment, caution was the watch-word. When he caught up to them he wanted to be the one with the advantage of surprise.

Fortunately for Curly the first tinges of pink were beginning to stain the morning sky as he left the settlement behind. The strengthening light made the hoofprints of his quarry an easy trail to follow. In the gentle heat of the awakening day he was aware of the faint scent of the late pasque flowers, people hereabouts called them 'prairie smoke'. Curly wasn't a superstitious man by nature, but the longer the perfume clung to his nostrils the greater the notion grew in his mind that this was some sort of premonition; that the smoke on the prairie this morning would be gunsmoke.

Twenty minutes later, breasting a small rise, he was surprised to see a riderless horse grazing on a ridge some quarter of a mile ahead. He hadn't expected them to stop so soon, but nor had he expected them to head in this direction when they left Laramie. They had diligently declared their intention of seeking work as drovers in Wyoming. This wasn't the way to Wyoming. They were heading south, back to the high-grass country, to Cheyenne or beyond to Denver.

He dismounted, led his horse into a thicket and tethered it out of sight. Again he checked his guns. Satisfied, he scampered over the undulating meadow to where he'd last seen the horse. By now it was out of sight, grazing, Curly hoped, on the far side of the ridge, for he hadn't heard any sound to suggest his quarry had ridden away.

He bellied his way to the edge, removed his hat and looked over. The land beyond had formed a kind of saucer-shaped depression, the bottom being some twenty feet below the point where Curly lay. The horse he had seen earlier had wandered down to the bottom and stood patiently alongside a second animal, neither of them showing any interest in the activity that was taking place close by. A wide-spreading cottonwood reached up from the bottom of the depression and at the foot of the tree Lew Butler and Charlie Huntz were eagerly shifting rocks. Occasionally their voices could be heard but the words were unclear.

Cautiously, Curly squirmed forward, using any cover available that got him closer to the pair. There were few rocks large enough to hide his big frame and the grass was no more than knee high, but he kept going until he'd reached a point just a few feet away. All the way down from the ridge he'd been afraid they would hear him crawling through the grass or dislodging a stone. Now his main concern was that they would hear him breathing. He was no longer a young man and, as a resident agent, it had been many years since he'd last been active in apprehending outlaws.

The tension of the situation was taking its toll. He was breathing shallowly and frequently though he was telling himself to breathe slowly and deep. In his head the sound of his breathing was like a timber saw in the forest. He lay still, not wanting to reveal his presence until Lew Butler and Charlie Huntz had finished their excavation.

The possibility that they were under surveillance never occurred to Lew and Charlie. Their concentration was entirely focused on the pile of boulders they were shifting one by one. With that task accomplished, Charlie retrieved a short-handled shovel from the pack behind his saddle. He offered it to Lew, who leant with his back against the cottonwood, wiping his brow with his shirt sleeve.

'Get on with it,' he told Charlie.

Charlie Huntz scooped out a shovelful of soil and spread it on the ground behind him. He dug again and again. Six times the shovel lifted out dirt, and on the seventh it struck the saddle-bags that he'd buried there some days earlier.

'Here they are!' His voice held an edge of excitement as though he were discovering a treasure that had been lost for years. He flung the shovel aside and reached into the hole he'd created. He tugged and tugged, and, when the pouches failed to come up freely, scrabbled in the dirt with his bare hands to clear away the impediment. He stood up and swung the well-filled saddle-bags to shake off the clinging soil. He opened one side and withdrew a bundle of banknotes.

'We gonna divide it now?' he asked.

Lew pushed himself away from the tree and stood beside his partner.

'Tonight,' he said, 'when we make camp. I'd like to put a bit more distance between us and that Wells Fargo agent before we're missed.'

'Too late for that.' Curly got to his feet. There was a nervous timbre to his voice but his rifle was held steadily in his hands.

Charlie made a move for the revolver at his side. Curly swung the rifle so that it covered him.

'If you give me cause I'll plug you,' he declared. 'Those men you killed were my friends so I don't need much encouragement to pull this trigger.'

Charlie let his hand relax.

'Now, without making any sudden moves,' continued Curly, 'unfasten your gunbelts and let them fall at your feet.'

Lew Butler spoke. 'You're smarter than I gave you credit for,' he told Curly. 'It was the hat, wasn't it? That's what put you on to us, I reckon.'

Curly didn't answer, just kept his gun pointed towards them.

'Figured you recognized it last night.

Must say, though, I didn't think you'd watch for us leaving town. Wells Fargo must be mighty proud to have a man like you looking after their interest.'

'Quit talking,' said Curly, 'and drop those guns.'

While he'd been talking Lew had moved slowly to his left, increasing the gap between himself and Charlie Huntz, making it more difficult for Curly to keep them both covered.

'Stand still,' the Wells Fargo agent ordered, 'and drop those guns. I won't tell you again.'

'Sure, sure. Don't get edgy. Charlie, throw him the saddle-bags.'

Charlie lobbed the leather pouches into the air and they landed near Curly's feet. Lew took the opportunity to move a few more steps, getting further from Charlie and nearer the grazing horses.

'Stand still,' ordered Curly, less sure now that he was in control of the situation, not sure whether to point the gun at Lew or Charlie. 'And for the last time of asking, drop that gun.'

'OK OK' Lew unfastened the buckle and let the belt and weapon fall to the ground.

With one man unarmed, Curly concentrated on the other outlaw.

'Now you.'

Charlie unfastened his belt slowly, menacingly exuding some sort of confidence that he could still draw and shoot the Wells Fargo man before he could pull the trigger. It was a ploy, of course: keeping Curly distracted while Lew moved more quickly towards the horses. When Charlie's gun hit the ground Lew needed only three more steps. Out of the corner of his eye, Curly caught the movement and pivoted to his right to shoot Lew.

It was too late. One of the horses was now between him and his target. Charlie shouted, not words: something like a Rebel yell. Nervously, Curly swung his rifle so that it now covered his other prisoner. Curly's indecision was what Lew had been waiting for. He drew his rifle from its saddle scabbard, threw himself to the ground and fired up from under the horse's body. Curly took two slugs in the chest and crumpled to the ground. Without another thought for their victim, Lew and Charlie gathered up their guns and money, clambered on their horses and rode away.

10

The experiences of the past few days had left Ellie Rogers in a state of shock.

Barely a word passed her lips as she and Wes rode at a canter towards Fort Laramie. After half an hour Wes gave up trying to make conversation, but he watched her closely. Her discomfort, he realized, was not only mental but physical, too. Continuously she tugged at her ill-fitting clothes, adjusted the collar of the shirt one minute, clamping a hand to the floppy-brimmed hat which threatened to part company with her head the next and, intermittently, tugged at the waistband of Jim Taylor's old wool trousers which rolled over the rope belt that Wes had fashioned for her.

In addition, despite the assurances she had given him that she was a capable horsewoman, she seemed ill at ease in the saddle and had difficulty maintaining the easy pace at which they travelled. Wes wondered if she was more accustomed to riding sidesaddle.

Wes loved the surrounding country. The meadow-land was lush and the tree-lined lower slopes of the hills abounded in game. Mildwater Creek never ran dry. Constantly fed by the melting high-ground snow, it provided a year-round water supply for the valley, and its nearby convergence with the South Platte provided an alternative water route to the larger eastern settlements. Yes, it was good land, a site on which a man could settle, raise stock and plant crops.

These were thoughts that had dwelt in Wes Gray's mind ever since he'd first come across this valley. That had been eight years ago, at a time when he'd known he wasn't ready to put down roots in one spot. The frontier land was too big, the horizon too challenging for him to dismount at the same spot every night. Then he'd shown the valley to

Jim Taylor and it seemed that the potential of the valley for raising stock had occurred as instantly to him as it had to Wes himself. When Jim declared his intention of leaving the wagon train and settling on the V of land it pleased Wes to know that the valley was in the hands of a friend who would work it wisely and efficiently.

That wasn't the way it had worked out. Now Jim Taylor was dead and thoughts of ownership once more niggled at Wes. They were stronger this time. Perhaps the dreams of those settlers he had guided to their own promised land were beginning to rub off on him. Also there was Sky. Common law decreed that the land was hers but, even as Jim's ex-wife, it was a claim that would never stand up in a court of law. Indians had no rights in American courts and their marriage had been blessed only by the Sioux. Anyone happening upon this valley now could claim the land as their own. Apo Hopa would be chased from it, chased back without recompense to the village of her people.

It occurred to Wes that perhaps he thought about Apo Hopa more than he did about the land. Remembrance of her prettiness tinged with an inner sadness warmed him as he rode. He attributed the sadness to Jim Taylor's behaviour. Yet she hadn't left him, as she so easily could have done, though whether she stayed because of love or loyalty he couldn't say. It wasn't always easy to tell with Indian girls. Knowing that she had been allowed to marry Jim Taylor so that a bond of friendship could be forged between the Ogallalah and the Americans would have been justification enough for Apo Hopa to put aside her own unhappiness and stay with her husband. It also occurred to Wes that her people might have killed him a long time ago if she hadn't stayed.

That Apo Hopa liked him, Wes, she had made abundantly clear. He could still feel the softness of her lips on his when they had kissed an hour earlier. She would be a good wife for him, a woman who would make him accepted among the Sioux in the same way as Little Feather made him a brother of the Arapaho. Neither woman would be jealous of the other. It wasn't their way. When he lived with her people, Little Feather expected him to be faithful to her, but he lived with them for less than three months each year; a great warrior like Medicine Feather needed a woman at other times. Little Feather understood this, so would Sky.

In addition, he reasoned with himself, uniting himself with the Sioux was the best way of ensuring the safety of the wagons he guided through their territory. He would become more fluent in their tongue, more familiar with their habits and, just as he did for the Arapaho, he would speak on their behalf at negotiation meetings with the authorities. With his mind thus engaged he rode silently towards Fort Laramie.

When Red started tossing his head

and coughing out an occasional snicker Wes's attention was drawn to more immediate matters. The horse had sensed something that had escaped the scout's notice. In this undulating country with plenty of tree cover it would probably be the presence of Indians. Wes scanned the tree line but saw nothing. The hairs on his neck made his skin itch in the way it did when his senses were on full alert. He was sure that someone was watching, following them, but keeping well out of sight.

The thought that the watchers were Sioux troubled Wes. Everything depended on the outcome of last night's council. If Black Raven was the new chief, or if he now led a breakaway band, then Wes's life and Ellie's were at risk. Wes reached across and grabbed the bridle of the horse that carried Ellie Rogers.

'Let's see if we can pick up the pace a bit,' he told her. 'The sooner I get you to the fort the sooner I can head back to the wagons.' It was an excuse to get out of the high-grass country as quickly as possible, though not without an element of truth.

Ellie made no reply. Her grip on the leathers tightened, as did the firm set of her mouth. The look in her eyes was one of alarm, as though she disbelieved him, but her thighs gripped against the saddle and her body leant forward in anticipation of the gallop.

Wes didn't put Red to a full gallop, but for ten minutes they maintained a brisk pace. Every so often he threw glances to right and left of him, wherever he spotted a likely rise, a grove of trees or an outcrop of rock that would be a suitable observation point for anyone watching them. No one appeared. Any watchers, he began to tell himself, had been just that, and had never had any other intention. He hoped it was a good sign, that Red Knife's view had prevailed and he was still chief in the village.

When they slowed again to a walk,

Ellie Rogers fussed once more with her makeshift wardrobe. She pulled the hat higher on her head so that its brim didn't flop in her eyes and, at the same time, showed more of her face to Wes. He inspected her for a while, taking note of the small scrapes and discoloration on her cheeks and jaw. Ellie noticed his examination.

'Fell in the river,' she explained. 'Trying to escape.' She paused for a moment, looked down at her hands clasped on the saddle horn. 'He wasn't too gentle with me but I won't die.'

'Any other injuries?' He'd watched the way she'd sat uneasily astride the mare, wondering if he was mistaken in his original conjectures about her horsemanship. Perhaps the awkwardness was due to damage he couldn't see, not because she was accustomed to riding sidesaddle.

Her eyes met his, sensitive of the question he was asking; she was coy with her answer even though, at first, it was nothing more than a slight shake of her head. After a moment she added,

'The Indians attacked almost as soon as he'd dragged me on to the bank. He was the first one they killed. The other two fled. I expect the Indians killed them, too.'

'Can you describe them?'

Wes's question went unanswered. Before Ellie could speak two riders came over a rise immediately ahead.

At first Wes thought they might be soldiers, part of a troop on patrol in the hills. But that thought lasted only an instant. These two were riding too quickly, like men who needed to be somewhere quickly, or wanted to be away from somewhere in a hurry. When the riders were a hundred yards away they pulled their horses to a slithering halt, one of them executing a full circle as he brought his animal under control. The size of them, their shape, the red hair and bushy beard of one and the long, lank hair of the other straggling down from beneath a wide-brimmed, gleaming white hat were enough to identify them as the men he had last seen in Clancy's bar in the Laramie settlement. If confirmation were needed it came from the girl to his left. Ellie gasped. Wes asked the question.

'Know them?'

'Yes.'

'Are they the men who robbed the stagecoach?'

'Yes.'

'Then you'd better ride into those trees. Get out of the line of fire.'

Quick though Wes and Ellie had been to recognize the outlaws, Lew Butler and Charlie Huntz had been just as quick to recognize the two people on the trail ahead of them. Although they were amazed that either Ellie or Wes were still alive, that didn't impinge on their reactions when it came to self-survival. Before Ellie could turn her mount towards the slope to her left they had drawn their rifles and fired. Neither man hit his target but the gunfire spurred Wes and Ellie to ride hard for the protection of the trees.

210

Bullets flew around them as they rode but none came close enough to damage either horses or riders. Lew and Charlie threw plenty of lead but neither thought to pause long enough to take careful aim. By the time such an idea occurred to Lew the targets were zigzagging between the trees and no clear shot was available.

'We've got to finish them this time,' he told Charlie, and they rode up the slope in pursuit.

Wes Gray's mind was occupied with a similar thought. The two men firing at him had caused enough trouble and had to be stopped. He glanced behind and spotted them still some thirty yards from the trees. As he rode deeper among the dense collection of hillside pines he looked for suitable cover from where he could better resist their attack. A double stand of tall trees surrounded by chest-high bushes and knee-high ground foliage seemed to offer what he sought. In addition to protection, it gave him the advantage of high ground. From there he would be able to oversee any manoeuvre of his adversaries.

He reined in, jumped from the saddle and with one hand pulled his rifle from its saddle boot. With the other hand he dragged Ellie from her horse. Letting go of her for an instant, he slapped the hindquarters of both horses, urging them further up the hill and using their movement as a decoy.

'Not a sound,' he said to Ellie as, grabbing her arm again, he moved her towards the shelter of the high bushes.

She was shivering or, more accurately, quaking. For the first time since the shooting had begun he looked at her. Her face had lost all its colour, her eyes were wide and her lips trembled. Low in her throat a sound rumbled, uncontrolled, unintelligible. Fear was evolving into panic. Any moment now, Wes knew, she would scream and that scream would not only remove the element of surprise, his main advantage, but would also pinpoint their location to the oncoming outlaws. He punched her on the jaw and she collapsed, senseless, in his arms.

Swiftly he laid her on the ground between the trees and thick bushes. There she was obscured from sight and safe from stray bullets. He threw some fern fronds on top of her for extra camouflage, hoping she wouldn't regain her senses until the fight was finished. A bullet whistled near his head and embedded itself with a thunk into a tree behind. Wes wasn't sure if it had been a lucky shot or if he had compromised his position by gathering up the fronds with which he'd covered the girl. He chanced a look between the trees.

Lew Butler and Charlie Huntz had dismounted. Charlie had his rifle at his shoulder and Wes pulled back behind the tree trunk as the trigger was pulled. The bullet sliced a huge slick of wood from the pine close to Wes's head. If the first shot had been close by chance, the second definitely had not. They knew where he was and now unleashed a fusillade towards the bushes and trees he was using as cover.

Sparingly, Wes returned their fire. Two shots, neither fired with the expectation of hitting a target, were simply a by-play to give him a moment in which to think. His first need was to draw the outlaws away from Ellie. She had neither the means nor the ability to defend herself. If she fell into their hands they would show no mercy.

Some six or seven yards to his right, a little further up the hill, a fallen tree offered him the cover he needed to take the fight to the enemy. If he could reach that tree he would be able to use the surrounding undergrowth to crawl away unseen in any direction, but the gap between it and where he was now was an open glade; he would be a clear target if he attempted to cross it. He needed to give himself an advantage, find some way of distracting them while he made the dash further uphill. He elected to use a simple tactic, one he had used several times in the past.

Crouching low, gripping his rifle in his left hand he prepared for the uphill run. He took his hat in his right hand and skimmed it low so that it wasn't seen by those below until it emerged, mere inches above the ground, from the bushes behind which Ellie lay. Gunfire roared and bullets flew towards the scout's hat.

Meanwhile Wes took his chance, running at a crouch in the opposite direction, finally throwing himself over the fallen tree. In the last two strides slugs dug up chunks of earth and smashed into wood as his headlong dash was spotted. The discomfort he experienced from his chest and head wounds when he hit the ground made him grimace, but he was still able to turn it into a grin as he rolled himself tight against the trunk.

'Got you,' he said, confident that his adversaries were no match for him in the wood.

He crawled to the further end of the

fallen tree before taking a look down the hill to see what the outlaws were doing. For the moment they were lost from sight but Wes could see their horses, ground hitched just below the tree line. He scanned the area as best he was able without exposing himself to the gunmen. He expected gunfire to be aimed in his direction at every moment but nothing happened. Looking back to where he'd left Ellie Rogers he detected no movement. As yet she hadn't regained consciousness, for which he was grateful.

A second scan among the trees brought him some reward. Lew and Charlie had split up, Charlie working his way uphill off to the right and Lew to the left, stopping for cover at every tree. They were executing a pincer movement. With their positions fixed in his mind, Wes crawled higher up the slope through the long grass. After two or three minutes he stopped and, using a tree with a particularly wide girth for cover, stood.

He scoured the hillside for movement. There was none. The outlaws were more stealthy than he had expected, perhaps more accustomed to hunting than he had earlier given them credit for. He stood and listened. There was only silence. The birds and animals of the wood had stopped their normal work to witness the violence of men. He waited. He watched. He listened. There was nothing to see. Nothing to hear. The place where he'd left Ellie was undisturbed; he wasn't sure how much longer that would last. She would soon be recovering her senses, stirring, making a noise that would attract the attention of the killers.

Wes Gray waited another minute; then, when still nothing moved, he decided it was time to become the hunter. He propped his rifle against the big pine and dropped to his knees. At that moment he heard a sound, a soft drumming of hoofbeats. Suspecting that something had driven away his pursuers he chanced a look around the tree. The outlaws' horses were still ground-tied where he had last seen them, which meant that someone else was riding the trail.

Perhaps a posse or a cavalry troop were out searching for Ellie Rogers. Lew Butler and Charlie Huntz, he reckoned, had already spotted them and were lying low, hoping their pursuers would pass by without becoming aware of the nearness of their prey. It would be a simple matter for Wes to destroy their plan. One gunshot would do it.

On reflection, Wes hesitated to take such action. The killers' horses were tethered below the tree line, their presence apparent to anyone near by. No posse or army patrol would ride by without investigating. But the sound of the hoofbeats was now receding; whoever had passed by had shown no inclination to discover the identities of the riders of the grazing horses, so they weren't likely to involve themselves in trouble if they heard the sound of gunfire.

Wes also reasoned that not only would that gunfire not bring back the unknown riders: it would also give away his position to those he was about to hunt. He withdrew his knife and began to snake through the grass, downhill, in a wide arc to his right.

Charlie Huntz was the first one he found. He lay, unmoving in long grass. When Wes slithered alongside him he saw that someone had got to Charlie before him. His eyes stared sightlessly at the sky, his shirt was bloody, covering a chest caved in by a series of hatchet blows and his red-haired scalp had been taken. The Sioux had taken their revenge for the deaths of Pony Holder and Little Otter. The sensation that Wes had experienced earlier, that Ellie and he were being watched, had not been imagination. They had been followed but it could only be that Red Knife was still chief of the Ogallalah village and that they were under his protection.

That protection hadn't extended to Lew Butler and Charlie Huntz. Wes found Lew Butler a few minutes later. His fate had been similar to Charlie's, except that his death blows had been delivered by the knife that had taken his hair.

When he got back to the bushes where he'd left Ellie Rogers, Wes found her stumbling around on unsteady feet. Concussion and a sore jaw, combined with the belief that she was alone in a strange and dangerous land, were causing panic to mount within her. When Wes stepped into sight her nerves were so taut that she screamed.

'Nothing more to worry about,' he told her. 'Those men are dead.'

He didn't tell her how they'd died, nor that he'd dropped their bodies into a narrow crevice where he hoped they wouldn't be found for a hundred years. He couldn't take the mutilated bodies back to Fort Laramie because he didn't want the authorities to know they'd been killed by the Sioux. As with Jim

Taylor, even though the white men had committed the first crime and deserved to die, the truth of their death would only lead to trouble for the Indians. Everyone would be happy if they thought he had killed them for robbing the stagecoach and kidnapping the girl.

Wes rounded up the horses, retrieved his rifle and hat, then helped Ellie back into the saddle. Comforted by the knowledge that her ordeal was over, she regained a little of her composure and managed a brief smile. After attaching the lead reins of the ground-tethered horses to his saddle horn he checked the contents of the bulging saddle-bags slung across their backs. He wasn't the least bit surprised to find them full of bundles of paper money — the proceeds, he figured, of the robbery.

As they rode away towards the fort Wes turned in the saddle and looked back towards the Mildwater Creek country. On a ridge, a single Indian sat astride his pony, watching their progress. The wind ruffled his long hair and the mane of his pony. He held a small round shield in his left hand and a long lance in his right. The feathers and decorations with which they were adorned also danced in the wind. It was Throws The Dust, Sky's brother. Wes raised his arm in salute.

They had been travelling for almost an hour when Wes spotted a riderless horse below the rim of a ridge off to his right.

'Wait here,' he told Ellie Rogers before making a detour to investigate. He approached cautiously lest the horse was skittish and ran off, but the bay mare watched him with nothing more than curiosity. Satisfied that the horse was sound he began to search for its owner. There were boot marks leading to the top of the ridge, so, drawing his gun, Wes began the climb.

His first impression was that the man who lay near the cottonwood tree on the floor of the depression was dead. Scurrying down the slope he quickly reached the prone figure and gently raised his shoulders to see his face.

'Curly!' he exclaimed. As the word hung in the air the Wells Fargo agent slowly opened his eyes. Relieved to find that the man still lived, Wes settled him on the ground once more and ran back to the top of the ridge. He signalled to Ellie, who rode over to join him. Meanwhile he collected his water canteen from his saddle and rushed back to where Curly lay.

It was a miracle that Curly Clayport was still alive; Wes suspected it would be another miracle if he survived the journey to Laramie, but he knew there was no alternative but to get him to a doctor. So the remainder of the journey to the fort was a slow affair. Curly was unable to ride alone, Wes sat behind him to make sure he didn't fall. But despite the pain and the weakness through loss of blood, Wes's news cheered Curly. News of dead road agents and the recovery of money and passenger were the best medicine he could get.

11

It was late afternoon when Fort Laramie came into view as the trio rode over the plain. Their slow, unsteady passage brought many of the Laramie Loafers from their tepees and those same Indians followed silently in their wake right up to the door of the commanding officer. By the time the horses were pulled to a halt news of their arrival had spread throughout the encampment and a large group of soldiers and civilian helpers had joined with the Indians to hear the news at first hand. Before the identities of the new arrivals was known, the immediate gossip was that they were survivors of some violent incident; more than one of those gathered in front of the camp office voiced the opinion that the expected Sioux uprising had begun.

It was little wonder that the populace

of the fort should believe that a battle had been fought because the three stricken riders were having difficulty in staying in the saddle: all were slumped forward as though injured or wounded. Curly Clayport was unconscious, his chin touched his chest, which was bound tightly with strips of his own bloodied shirt.

Behind him, his arms aching with the effort of holding on to the Wells Fargo agent, Wes Gray's gaunt expression gave testimony to the exertions of the day. Under Apo Hopa's ministrations, the wounds he'd sustained in the Sioux village had begun to heal; gashes had begun to smart as new skin bridged the gaps but now they burned like branding-scars, as though with every sudden movement they were being ripped open.

He'd endured them from the moment he'd thrown himself over the fallen tree when trading gunshots with Lew Butler and Charlie Huntz. Carrying their bodies to the rocky

crevice in which he'd deposited them
had added to his discomfort and the
pain had begun in earnest when he'd
lifted Curly on to Red. From that
moment every quick movement and
every stretch to ease his muscles had
sent a spasm of pain across his back.
Now he welcomed the hands that
reached up to ease Curly Clayport
from his grasp. People in the crowd
began voicing their recognition of the
men.

'It's Curly Clayport,' said one. 'He
looks bad. Better get him to the
hospital.'

'Hey! Wes Gray,' called another.
'What happened, Wes? Was it Sioux?'

An officer-like voice issued a command:

'Sergeant, get the colonel.'

Wes recognized the speaker as a
lieutenant who'd been stationed at
Laramie for several years.

'Come on into the office, Wes,' the
officer continued. 'You can tell your
story in there.'

Wes shifted in the saddle, suppressed a groan as he prepared to dismount, then caught sight of Ellie Rogers, who had been silent all the way from the depression where Curly Clayport had been shot. She was sort of hunched, her shoulders pushed forward and her head bowed as though she were closely inspecting her hands as they rested on her saddle. The big, soft, floppy grey hat hid most of her face and, because she wasn't known to the people of the fort, no one had paid a great deal of attention to her.

'Better help the girl down,' Wes told the lieutenant.

'Girl?' Wes saw the soldier and several others in the crowd look at Ellie with more interest. The ill-fitting clothes had effectively obscured her gender.

'Better find Captain O'Malley,' advised Wes. 'He'll want to know his fiancée is here.'

Murmurs in the crowd carried a tone of surprise at the news that O'Malley's girl had been found, but one voice, that of a woman, rose above the others as Ellie was helped from her horse. It was Mrs Flint, the colonel's wife, taking charge of the girl, insisting she must stay in the colonel's quarters until the doctor had examined her.

Colonel Flint poured whiskey for himself and Wes while the story was told.

'There's no Sioux uprising,' Wes began, which were exactly the words Colonel Flint wanted to hear. 'Lew Butler, Charlie Huntz and a third man held up the stage. They rode south, towards the North Platte, where they were attacked by a band of Shoshones . . .'

'Shoshones?' interrupted Colonel Flint.

'Probably the raiding party I'd seen that same day. I expect they wouldn't have attacked if Miss Rogers hadn't been with them. A white woman would be quite a prize to take back to their village.'

Colonel Flint nodded his understanding.

'But everyone agrees that the ponies those men rode in on belonged to the Sioux,' he observed.

'After the fight with the Shoshone, Lew Butler and Charlie Huntz lost their own horses. They came across a couple of Sioux boys, killed them and stole their horses.'

The soldier's eyebrows rose. He knew that any outrage against the Sioux could lead to war.

Wes placated him, told him about the death of Kicking Bear and that the new chief, Red Knife, wanted to maintain the peace with the Americans. He also told him that it was a Sioux warrior, Throws The Dust, who had rescued Ellie Rogers and taken her to his sister for safety.

'His sister was married to Jim Taylor. Jim is dead. Fell from a hayloft and broke his neck. I was there when it happened. I buried him.'

'He had a reputation,' said Colonel Flint. 'Not a good one. Too much whiskey.'

Wes nodded as though confirming that Jim Taylor had been drunk when he fell from the hayloft.

'And Curly? What happened to him?'

'He hasn't said anything yet,' replied Wes. 'I reckon he was suspicious of Lew Butler and Charlie Huntz and followed them out to that place where they shot him. I've got the money they stole. Perhaps you should hang on to it until someone from Wells Fargo shows up to claim it.'

He finished his whiskey then went to the hospital to enquire after Curly's injuries.

Wes remained overnight at the fort even though his sense of duty told him that he had already been absent from the wagon train for too long. His conscience, however, was untroubled. What he'd undergone in the previous few days meant that the Sioux were not a threat to the travellers on the Oregon Trail and, before he'd become embroiled in Laramie's affairs, he'd travelled enough of the trail ahead to know that the wagons would not encounter any natural obstacles more serious than those that, as wagon master, Caleb Dodge, overcame on every journey.

When he rejoined the wagons Caleb would rant and threaten to cut his fee, but they would both know that it was all show. Caleb knew that Wes did his job, and also that there was no one better.

When morning came Wes looked into the army infirmary to see Curly Clayport. The Wells Fargo man was weak but awake and pleased to see the scout.

'I'm really grateful to you Wes, not just for getting me back here but for getting those men who did this to me. If ever I can do anything in return just let me know. There'll be a reward, of course,' he added. 'The company will be grateful for what you did, getting the girl back as well as the money.'

'It was Red Knife's people who found the girl,' Wes told him. 'They should get the reward for that.' The expression on Curly's face confirmed Wes's belief that such a thing would never happen. 'And you caught up with the robbers before I did.'

'Yeah, but they shot me. Besides, company employees can't claim rewards.' He threw a rueful look at Wes. 'Reckon I won't be a company employee much longer. The doc says those slugs will slow me down some. Perhaps I'm just ready for a rocker on a porch someplace.'

Wes's thoughts began to race.

'I know a porch you can sit on,' he said. He explained his ideas to Curly. 'Jim Taylor is dead,' he told him. 'Got too full of whiskey and fell out his hayloft.'

Curly barely registered surprise. It was the kind of death the people in the settlement had predicted for Jim.

'I was there,' Wes continued, 'and I buried him for his woman. Someday I'd kinda like to settle on that land myself. At the moment there's an itch in my britches that can only be salved with saddle leather. How about sitting on the spread for me? Build it up if you will. We'll be partners and you can use any reward money I'm due.'

'Are you serious?'

'Sure. I ask only one thing. Be neighbourly with the Sioux. Welcome them to the ranch. I intend to be their brother just as I am brother to the Arapaho.'

Until that moment Curly Clayport had viewed the prospect of no longer being useful to Wells Fargo as drawing a curtain on his life. By the time Wes Gray left him he was anxious to begin a new life as rancher, or farmer, or cattleman.

Leading the horses that had belonged to Lew Butler and Charlie Huntz, Wes rode to the settlement. He exchanged those mounts for the Indian ponies the outlaws had been riding when they first arrived and immediately rode out towards Red Knife's village.

All the village gathered to watch Wes

Gray's approach. They formed themselves into two facing rows, much as they had when he'd had to run their gauntlet. This time he wasn't being shown the way to the totem pole and torture but to the tepee of Red Knife. Before it, beside the chief, stood Black Raven and Pawnee Killer. All three wore feathered bonnets and carried long, decorated lances. Wes kept his gaze straight ahead, holding the iron-eyed looks of the three warriors. During the final strides he sensed the presence of someone walking alongside him. A hand clutched a handful of his buckskin leggings, a symbol that Sky, whose hand he knew it to be, was declaring to the village that she had chosen him, as was the right of a widow, to be her next husband. It was a good sign for Wes, for it surely meant that he was not considered an enemy.

He halted and held out the lead reins of the Indian ponies he had brought with him. With a mixture of Sioux words and signs he told Red Knife and his people that he came among them with the hope of friendship.

'I return the ponies of Little Otter and Pony Holder,' he told them, 'and give you the news that the white men who killed them are now dead.' At this point Black Raven moved his lance slightly but distinctly so that the feathers and trophies attached to it fluttered and rattled against the shaft. Topmost of the trophies was a scalp of red hair — once it had been Charlie Huntz's. Likewise, Pawnee Killer's lance bore the scalp of Lew Butler. Wes gave each man a nod of acknowledgement.

'The soldiers at the fort believe that I killed those men. They will not come here to punish the Sioux.' Red Knife said the news he brought was good and invited him to smoke a pipe. Wes stepped down from Red and entered the chief's lodge.

Later, as he prepared to leave the village, Throws The Dust told Wes how he had seen Black Raven and Pawnee Killer watching as he took the white woman to the fort.

'Anger still drove their thoughts but I didn't think they would disobey Red Knife and attack you. When I saw your fight among the trees I recognized the man with red hair and the other one as the two who had fought the Shoshone. You told me they were the two men who had killed Pony Holder and Little Otter. I pointed them out to their fathers.'

'It was justice, Throws The Dust.'

'Yes. Black Raven and Pawnee Killer may never be your friend,' he said, 'but they are no longer your enemy. They were pleased you returned the ponies.'

'I must go,' Wes told him. 'Soon a new man will live in the cabin that was your sister's home. He is a good man. He will welcome and help your people.'

'And my sister,' he asked. 'What of her?'

'For now she must live in her father's tepee. When I return she will live in the lodge of Medicine Feather, brother of the Arapaho, friend of the Sioux.'

We do hope that you have enjoyed reading this large print book.

Did you know that all of our titles are available for purchase?

We publish a wide range of high quality large print books including:
Romances, Mysteries, Classics
General Fiction
Non Fiction and Westerns

Special interest titles available in large print are:
The Little Oxford Dictionary
Music Book, Song Book
Hymn Book, Service Book

Also available from us courtesy of Oxford University Press:
Young Readers' Dictionary
(large print edition)
Young Readers' Thesaurus
(large print edition)

For further information or a free brochure, please contact us at:
Ulverscroft Large Print Books Ltd.,
The Green, Bradgate Road, Anstey,
Leicester, LE7 7FU, England.
Tel: (00 44) **0116 236 4325**
Fax: (00 44) **0116 234 0205**

VALERON'S RANGE

Terrell L. Bowers

When Scarlet Valeron, poised to be married in Pueblo, Colorado, is kidnapped and her betrothed killed, a desperate call goes out to the Valeron family. Brothers, cousins, and hired help unite in an effort to find her and bring her back. They learn Scarlet is on her way to Brimstone, a bandit stronghold of over a hundred outlaws. Most would look at the incredible odds and figure Scarlet was lost forever. The Valerons, however, see it as a matter of family honour to get their kin back, and settle the score!

DEVINE'S MISSION

I. J. Parnham

When Lachlan McKinley raids Fairmount Town's bank, the bounty on his head attracts plenty of manhunters — but everyone who goes after him ends up dead. When bounty hunter Jonathon Lynch, Lachlan's stepbrother, joins the hunt, he soon discovers that all is not as it seems, and Lachlan may in fact be innocent. Worse, US Marshal Jake Devine is also after Lachlan. Devine is more likely to destroy the peace than to keep it, so can Jonathon bring the guilty to justice before Devine does his worst?

PERIL ON THE OREGON TRAIL

Billy Hall

Hannah Henford, travelling west aboard a steamer, meets the reticent young Andrew Stevenson, who captures her heart with his bravery when the boat docks and they embark upon the Oregon Trail. Jeremiah Smith, a mysterious and adventurous mountain man, discovers Hannah alone and takes her in search of wild turkeys. She cannot help but be charmed by Jeremiah, but he may not be all that he seems. In Arapaho territory, Andrew will be needed again: in pursuit of Hannah, he will face peril on the Oregon Trail.

THE VIGILANCE COMMITTEE WAR

Bill Sheehy

A gang of vigilantes calling themselves the Vigilance Committee are preventing part of the Indian Territory from becoming a state, and former Texas Rangers Buck Armstrong and Louie Lewis are being paid by local businesses to bring them in. Making their job difficult is the fact that most of the area's ranchers don't care, or approve of the hangings carried out by the Committee. When the pards get too close to Committee members, Louie himself ends up at the end of a hangman's noose . . .

ALONG THE TONTO RIM

Will DuRey

Dick Lazarus and his gang are feared on both sides of the Rio Grande. Lazarus's increasingly daring crimes see him raid the ranchero of the Robles family in Mexico, stealing a herd of horses and taking a hostage — Luis Robles — who should fetch a hefty ransom. Dan Calloway, owner of the stolen herd and Luis's friend, is determined to rescue Luis and regain his possessions. Ignoring the warnings, and with an unexpected ally on his side, he pursues Lazarus across the Rio Grande, and along the Tonto Rim . . .